RUNNING BEAR

BEAR

*Grandson of
Red Snake*

Books by George McMullen

Red Snake

One White Crow

Running Bear

RUNNING BEAR

Grandson of Red Snake

George McMullen

HAMPTON ROADS
PUBLISHING COMPANY, INC.

Cover art by John Edens
Illustrations by Daniel Burstein
Cover design by Marjoram Productions

For information write:

Hampton Roads Publishing Company, Inc.
134 Burgess Lane
Charlottesville, VA 22902
Or call: (804)296-2772
FAX: (804)296-5096

If you are unable to order this book from your local
bookseller, you may order directly from the publisher.
Quantity discounts for organizations are available.
Call 1-800-766-8009, toll-free.

ISBN 1-57174-037-6

10 9 8 7 6 5 4 3 2 1

Printed on acid-free paper in Canada

I dedicate this book

to

Charlotte (Lottie)

My Wife, My Love, My Best Friend

for her help and encouragement always.

Contents

Foreword

On a sunny and windy day one spring, I met George McMullen for the first time, when he came to Helena, Montana, to apply his unusual skills to some half-buried stone rings on prairie land beneath snow-mottled peaks, just outside of town.

He walked across the meadow and stopped before two concentric stone rings, massaging a small stone in his hand. His gaze unfixed, his breath raspy, he stood quietly for a few minutes. Then he spoke in his gravelly voice. "I know what it is now." He went on to describe an initiation ceremony where young boys were kept in a tent, without clothes on, and brought one by one from one ring to the next. The movement from one stone circle to the next symbolized the movement from childhood to adulthood, and as each passed into the second ring a stone was moved with them. Each boy was tattooed and each was given a new name.

George's analysis was formed in a matter of minutes by simply picking up a rock from the site and *psychometrizing* it; that is, he held it and a very vivid replay of the past here came to him. George says he travels back to the past in his mind's eye and sees scenes like this unfolding as if, he says, he were there.

"I project myself up in the air," he says. "I'm looking down on what's going on below as if I were up in a helicopter or perhaps a tall tree." Once he has the scene, he says, he moves down to ground level. He can fast-forward or rewind. These scenes—such as the initiation ceremony—are as real as the present, sometimes more so. Smoke from the fire, he says, will cause his eyes to tear and make him sneeze.

Is this a real phenomenon? Does George travel back to the past to fetch scenes and other data that took place hundreds or thousands of years ago?

I don't know. On a gut level, I believe that George *is* able to travel backwards in time. So do many respected anthropologists who have been helped by George. So do some policemen who have used his talents. "There are plenty of phonies out there," said one police captain. "One thing George is not, is a phony." No one knows how it works, and it's far from perfect. It needs more study. It needs more investigation.

George says that his psychic informants—two women and a man—are best on matters concerning Native Americans. And so it would seem in these stories of Running Bear, the grandson of Red Snake, who was the subject of a book by his name. These stories of one man's life among the Huron Indians centuries ago are entertaining and intriguing. And who knows—they may well be telegrams from the past.

Jim Robbins

Preface

Taking a step backwards to a more spiritually sophisticated time, *Running Bear* opens the consciousness of modern man to an era when existence may have seemed raw, but also more basic and natural. The truth in the words provide a window into the hearts and minds of those whose lives and livelihoods were changing with the onset of the white settlers, a foreign presence whose habits and sensibilities were as distant as their native lands.

The author has, in his special way, brought emotional insight and a sense of reality to the life of Running Bear. This unique presentation is available to us only because George McMullen has the distinctive ability to actually view the path of this man and communicate with energies most of us never recognize. For lack of better terminology, George is, and always has been, psychic.

But, having known George for several years and having had the opportunity to work with him in Ecuador, I must state that *psychic*, in its understood form of definition, does not adequately describe the capabilities of this man. Perhaps the best identification can be found in the Greek word *psychikos*, which translates to "of the soul." The realm in which he works is in and of the souls of those who have long ago departed this plane of existence.

George's ability to *see* through the layers of our limited physical domain provides us an instrument in which we may traverse the dimension of time and space. His ability to *experience* forgotten moments in history, as they unfold with all of their joys and pains, gives to us a means with which we may emotionally identify with the subject. And his ability to *hear* presents to us words that are of the soul.

Running Bear is an extraordinary story as told through an extraordinary man and should be, in my opinion, viewed as a treasure. For it is a rare gift when we can see, experience, and hear the footsteps of a past that determined the path of the present and could, possibly, alter the direction of the future.

Britt Elders

Introduction

This is the life story of Running Bear, an Indian who lived at the time when the White Man "discovered" the New World. Born in the Huron village of Cahiague, he was the son of Three Eyes and the grandson of Red Snake. Three Eyes had joined Champlain's war against the Iroquois and had died in battle when Running Bear was a child. When the Mohawk raided their village in revenge, his mother and grandmother were killed. Red Snake took the boy to raise as his own, until he too was killed by a group of Mohawk warriors. As his grandmother had been a Mohawk, Running Bear was taken by the warriors to her people and raised by her family.

The account of Running Bear's life deals with the problems that faced the Indians with the coming of the White Man. His grandfather Red Snake was more generous than he toward the White Man, but Running Bear lived in a time when the number of White Men, and the disruptions they brought to the natives, was much greater.

Can you imagine a village of more than five thousand people being destroyed? The Huron sided with Champlain in his war against the Iroquois, but the French leader was defeated and barely escaped with his life. The Huron were then abandoned to their own fate when the

Iroquois took revenge on their village. But more devastating was the White Man's disease, which killed over two-thirds of the population of the Huron village.

Those who managed to escape both catastrophes moved away to be assimilated by other tribes. So the Huron Nation was no more, except for a few isolated camps, one of which still exists in the Province of Quebec but far from the original village.

Hereditary lines in the Huron Tribe and their cousins the Iroquois descended from the mother's side of the family. So it was natural that Running Bear be taken to the Mohawk, where his grandmother's people lived.

He did not want to become a Mohawk; he wanted to remain a Huron. He soon realized, however, that it did not matter—when the White people settled into his country, to them an Indian was an Indian. The White Man was interested only in the land, not the people occupying it.

Running Bear traveled the country around him, looking and hoping to find his place in it. He tried trapping and trading furs. For a while he even worked for a White man, but it was not to last; a situation arose wherein he had to kill the White man to protect himself.

When the White men arrived on these shores, their main interest was furs. But as time went on, many White people, both men and women, came to settle the land. As their numbers increased, more land was needed for them, and the Indian was forced from their hereditary hunting grounds.

As Running Bear traveled, he became more aware of the problems facing his people. He realized that he was powerless to do anything except try to survive the best way he knew how.

Eventually he settled down, working for a trader. He married a woman much younger than he and found happiness in his two sons. But his life was cut short when he, too, succumbed to the White Man's lung disease.

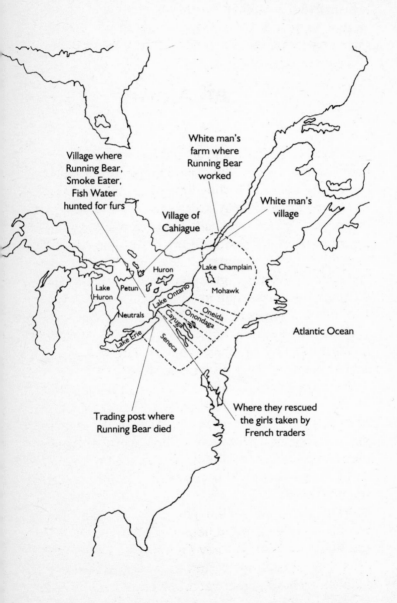

Village where
Running Bear,
Smoke Eater,
Fish Water
hunted for furs

White man's
farm where
Running Bear
worked

Village of
Cahiague

White man's
village

Lake Champlain

Huron

Lake Ontario

Mohawk

Lake
Huron

Petun

Oneida

Onondaga

Neutrals

Cayuga

Lake Erie

Seneca

Atlantic Ocean

Trading post where
Running Bear died

Where they rescued
the girls taken by
French traders

1. Left Alone

I heard Grandfather grunt and felt him fall on my back, pushing me to the ground under him. I knew something was very wrong, but I was confused. We had been walking all day, keeping to the lowlands and brush, through swamps and potholes. We knew the enemy was around us and Grandfather and I had kept our silence. I could now feel warmth on my back and hear Grandfather groaning under his breath. He was pulled roughly from my back, and as I looked up I could see a warrior grab his hair and pull back his head and hold a knife to his throat. A cry came from another of the Mohawk and the man holding Grandfather stopped his hand in surprise.

I was grabbed and pulled to my feet. I tried to get to Grandfather, but they held me away. I could see the arrows sticking out of his back. Two men were holding him from falling, as they lowered him to his knees and held him up. The oldest of the Mohawk spoke to him and told him they had not known it was Red Snake when they attacked us.

They asked what they could do for him, and through his pain he told them to care for me, and to see that I was taken to my Grandmother's people. This they agreed to do. They then placed him on a fallen branch, sitting up, yet draped over it, as he had requested. They put him facing onto the swamp toward the sunset. Blood was now running from his mouth and down his chest and there was a glazed look in his eyes. I knew my Grandfather was dying, and I was filled with pain and grief.

When I was born, I was called No Hair because I had no hair on my head at all. My grandmother had to make me a small fur hat to keep my head warm. I did not start to grow hair until I was around three years old. My mother and father thought I would be bald all my life so were happy when it finally began to grow.

My father's name was Three Eyes, and he was the son of Red Snake. He was killed fighting with the French against the Iroquois. It was after this that the Iroquois took vengeance on my people, who were the Huron. Many people were killed and their villages destroyed.

During an Iroquois raid on our village, they killed my mother and sister.

My grandmother, Fawn, had been killed by other women in the village in revenge for the raid, as she was a Mohawk and still lived as they did. She was the wife of Red Snake, my grandfather. When he returned to the village after her death, he was shocked by what his people had done so left the village for a while to recover from his grief and to decide his future. He had left me with friends, so now he had to make some arrangements to go on living for both our sakes. He decided to go into the territory of another tribe further to our north to escape the Iroquois.

We lived there by a waterfall and were joined by a woman who had been left there by these people. We cared for her and she for us. We stayed there for a little over two years. It was while we were at this place that Grandfather taught me about hunting and fishing and we became great friends. When I was about twelve years old, Grandfather decided that we should go to the Mohawk village of my grandmother's people, where he hoped I would again be able to enjoy a family life with others my own age.

This did not appeal to me, as I was content to stay the way we were. There was plenty of food and we had a nice place to live. The woman was good to us and worked hard to please us. Besides, we both knew the trip to the Mohawk village would be very dangerous, for we had heard the Iroquois were busy hunting down our people everywhere they could find them and would give us no peace.

But Grandfather would not change his mind about going, so we made plans to leave. I realized that he was now very old for our people, and his hearing and sight were not as good as they had been. He had been one of the great hunters of our village. He was known for his good nature and was generous to everyone. Many tales were told of his bravery when he was aroused, and stories of his love for his Mohawk wife were told by many a jealous woman in our tribe. He treated her so well that many women held it as an example to their men, which did not please them.

His way of living apart from the tribe, while still part of it, confused many who could not understand him. He did not join in the rituals, although none knew them better than he. He was respected by the chiefs and the Shaman, so they often sought out his council. He would not at any time join the war parties, but preferred his own company on the hunt. It was a good way for him, as he was the most successful hunter in our village. He had more skins and pelts than anyone else.

While hunting with him I learned his ways very well. If he was hunting deer he acted and thought like a deer, which he could do well because of his long association with them.

He did the same with the beaver and the bear, thinking and acting just as they would. His knowledge and understanding of the forest and of the creatures came from a lifetime of living among them. I listened to everything he said and tried to follow his example.

Grandfather did not have interest in things of the past any more, and I knew he wanted me to be where I was safe, before anything happened to him. So we left a safe and comfortable place and made our way south by southwest, being careful to keep away from known trails where people usually traveled. It was during this trip that disaster struck and took my grandfather away from me. He was more to me than any other person I have known.

I went to Grandfather and laid my head to his and he whispered for me to go with the Mohawk, and always remember I was a Huron and to be proud. Tears streamed down my face, mixing with his blood. He held me for a moment and then pushed me away. The older Mohawk took my arm and pulled me away from him. As we all left my grandfather, I looked back and could see him staring after us and then he turned his head and looked out toward the sinking sun.

We went about a hundred yards and made a camp. The warriors looked at me and talked among themselves. The older one told me they were very sorry for what had happened and they would see that he was buried with the respect due a great warrior. They said that they would take me to my grandmother's family, whom they knew well and would leave me there. They asked me to promise that I would not try to escape, so they could leave me untied, but if I tried to go they would have to bind me, as they had promised Red Snake to do as he asked, and they intended to keep their promise.

20

I agreed to stay and they left me. Soon they had a fire going and cooked food which I declined and went to my bed fur where I cried away the night. In the morning I swore I would never shed another tear the rest of my life and I never did. I went with them to bury my grandfather and they treated him with great respect.

2. My New Family

After everything had been attended to in custom and ceremonies for Grandfather, we left, heading toward the southwest. I immediately realized the difference when traveling with these men. They walked along without fear of attack and made much noise and loud talk. Grandfather and I had crept and hid, being careful to make no noise or fire, to keep unseen by the Iroquois. I found myself looking ahead and behind from habit. It was something I never did lose and it saved my life many times.

We were soon in the country of a large tribe of people called the Petuns, who lived near the Neutrals who were friends with our people. Grandfather knew them and had visited them many times. We had to stop and visit these people in the days ahead as we passed by their villages. They paid no attention to me and didn't even enquire who I was. I kept quiet and kept thinking how I could escape these men and return to my own village.

They never gave me a chance to leave or left me alone. It does not mean they were treating me badly, just watching me all the time. I tried to steal a weapon from people we met, but never succeeded. I wanted revenge for my grandfather's death and would remember these men.

They traded for tobacco with the Neutrals, as they had come this way to do. We went along by the great lake until we came to the northern end and the islands that would make it easy for us to cross over.

They found their own canoes, which they had hidden in brush by the shore. Loading everything, they took off across the bay to the first island. It took us two days to get over to the main shoreline on the south side of the lake. We then headed down a fast-flowing river to another quite large lake.

At the bottom of the lake we came to a village of Mohawk people. Two of the men stayed there while the others, along with some men of the village, took me to the southwest. Around the fire pit at night, the men talked endlessly of the White people who were now becoming more noticed in their country. They told of the villages that they were building by the big river and the enormous canoes with cloth sails that had brought them here.

It was because these Mohawk people had such a wide territory and traveled about so much, that they had met the White people and had come in contact with others that knew them. I had seen the ones who had come to my village, but could not really recall what they looked like. I was much too young and as a result never grasped what it would mean to my future and to our people.

We traveled for days and it was now getting cooler in the evenings. They made haste to get to our destination, so they could return to their own villages after getting me to mine. They talked also of a large force of their warriors meeting somewhere in my country to finish off the war that we had foolishly started with the White Man's help. I knew they wanted to get into the action for part of the spoils of war.

We finally arrived at a camp set up in a deep valley with a stream and a small waterfall. It was near the main trail to the largest water of salt. There were ten small lodges with two hundred people living there, as I was to learn later. It appeared that we were expected and they wasted no time in taking me to one of the lodges and presenting me to a man who, I was later told, was my grandmother's brother's son. He was a small man with a kindly face.

He spoke to me about his family and how much I was welcomed there. He hoped that he would become my father and I his son. He knew we had a lot of hard adjustments to make, but he felt we could overcome any problems. He had never known my grandmother, but had heard about her. He had heard all about my grandfather and my father.

He asked if I knew that the Hurons were still at war with his people and if I could understand what it was all about. I told him I knew. He then introduced me to his woman and his three daughters and a baby boy. They did not seem pleased to see me, especially the girls. They looked at me with disdain; the woman ignored me completely. I was taken to a place where I was to make my bed and then left alone.

They later called me for the evening meal and I realized that they had eaten first and I was left the scraps from their meal. The girls looked at me in contempt as I tried to scrape out enough to eat. I left the fire pit and returned to my bed fur and slept very lightly that night.

I awoke the next morning before light and left camp, going along the small stream away from the valley. It was not long before I came to a large swamp and, scouting the edge, looked for muskrat signs as grandfather had taught me.

I stopped one with an arrow and killed another with a club as it swam past my hiding place in the bulrushes. I also got a fat water bird by swimming underwater and grabbing it and breaking its neck. So I returned to the village that night with two muskrat and the bird. The rest of the family then realized I could supply my own food and did not need their charity.

3. Growing Up

During the rest of my stay with these people I was never really accepted as part of the tribe. I was twelve years of age when I arrived there and the others of my age made me most miserable. I avoided contact as much as possible with them. I spent long days in the forest around the village. Strange as it seems, I liked to run fast and steadily with the wind in my face, over long distances. It was not long before I was the fastest runner in the village and won most of the races that were held during ceremonial times within the village and others nearby.

When I had been there about six months I was cleaning a deer carcass and was helping the oldest girl by holding the legs while she chopped them off. Suddenly—by accident, I hope—the axe slipped and she cut the two longest finger tips off my right hand. The Shaman and women of the tribe bound and took care of my hand and I never made a sound. The pain was worse the next few months when I learned to use the hand again, as the ends of the two fingers were very tender. My fingers on that hand were nearly all the same length now. It did not handicap me much, but I never held game again for the girl or anyone else.

As I mentioned, they had called me No Hair when I was a baby. Now they called me Short Fingers. This was just a nickname. When I was officially named during my manhood ceremony a few years later, they called me Running Bear. After that, some called me Short Fingers Running Bear. This was quite a long name, but not as bad as some were called.

I hunted for my own food and did the chores that were expected of me, still keeping out of the way as much as possible. The girls still spent their time insulting me when they could, especially about my manhood. They were continually trying to mate with me, as mating was a very loose affair for these people. They just found someone who was willing and went ahead with it.

I was continually coming across people in and around the village going at it in the bushes. The younger adults seemed to do this just as a matter of entertainment. I had learned at an early age what it was about and had mated with several girls in my own village and when on hunting trips. I had learned from the girls in other villages of our tribe.

Mating was not discouraged in our customs; in fact, everyone did it and thought nothing of it. Any resulting children were accepted gladly by the father of the girl, if she was not married, or by her husband as his own. There were no illegitimate children in our time.

As for other young men, they did not want to be seen with me, although they admired my running speed and the fact that I gave the tribe a champion. Most of them did not abuse me in any way, but others tried to. I was beaten by many during my stay here, although I always fought as hard as I could. It was never a one-on-one proposition, but two or more who waylaid me.

I had taken to sleeping out in the forest, away from camp, in a quiet little place by a small stream. Doing this, I could get away early to hunt. One night I was jumped on and bound by a group of other boys, who carried me to the women's house and dumped me inside the doorway.

The women's house was where the women of the tribe go at a certain time of the month during their menstrual period, so as to be away from the rest of the people. It was a great insult to a man's pride to be anywhere near this house and a greater insult to be told that you belong there.

I lay there in the dark in anger. A woman stumbled over me and called to the other women to help. They pulled me out of the house and left me on the ground for the rest of the night. The next morning a group collected around me, making insults. Someone told my new father so he came and released me. He was very angry but not as angry as I was. I knew someone would pay for this.

4. My Revenge

I had recognized some of the boys who were responsible for the women's house episode. I knew that in time I would get my revenge. I picked up my sleeping furs and weapons and took off into the forest. I stayed there for over a week before returning to the village. I crept around to where most of the people went to swim. I then sat and waited for any of the boys whom I had recognized to appear. I saw two of them leave the water and start along the trail toward camp and so I hid myself in a clump of willows.

Soon they came along and the look of surprise when I jumped out of the willows was gratifying. I hit the bigger of the two on the head with my club before he knew what was happening and stunned him. I threw myself onto the other, my fists swinging, and it was great to feel them hitting his flesh. I did not stop until he was on his knees and then I turned to the other who was getting to his feet. I flayed away at him until he was unconscious. They lay there, their faces cut and bruised. They both had known who their attacker was and I was content to let them be.

I went into camp and told my foster father what I had done. He only smiled and said nothing, but I knew he was prepared now in case there were any complaints about my behaviour. I told him I still had a score to settle with the others.

Again I returned to the forest and this time I was followed by three older men. I assumed they were somehow related to the two I had beaten up and later this was confirmed. I walked along the trail pretending I did not know they were there. I could hear them hurrying to catch up to me and I took off, running as fast as I could go. I ran for about five miles, then turned left and ran two more miles. I then backtracked so as to get behind them.

I watched for their trail and when I found it, I could see that they had been running to catch me. I followed their trail until I could hear them ahead. They were eating and talking among themselves. I crept closer and watched them. Finally they decided to continue in pursuit and they hid some of their gear so as to proceed faster and then left.

I waited until they were out of earshot, then I took the things they had hidden. They were the furs they needed for sleeping and some food, pipes, and tobacco. I took everything to a small pond nearby and soaked them in water until they were saturated.

I then replaced them where they had been hidden. I knew they would track me back here so I left, as I knew they would get the message. I made a Huron sign on the ground to doubly infuriate them.

I knew it would take them some time to get back, so I walked the same way they had gone, following my trail. I knew they would give up trying to track me now. I went about ten miles further on and slept up in a tree just in case. The next morning I went off in a different direction for most of the day. I hunted the third day and was lucky enough to get a plump deer. I ate some and dressed the rest. It was still too much for me to carry very far. I lashed sticks together to make a travois and piled the meat on top and dragged it slowly behind.

That night I hung the meat in a tree and made camp nearby. I had a heavy meal and went to sleep right after. I was awakened by a noise. I rolled into a thicket so I could stay out of sight until I found out what it was.

I watched my camp, and in a moment a man, woman, and children entered the camp. I watched them for a while and decided they meant me no harm and called to them.

They looked at me in silence as I approached the fire pit. They then greeted me in a friendly fashion and I made them welcome. I put out as much meat as they could possibly consume. They showed their appreciation by eating almost all of it. Afterwards we sat by the fire and talked. I told them who I was and where I had come from.

They did not question that I was a Huron and seemed to know more than they said. The man was a very good person and his family were well-behaved. I was only thirteen now, having just passed my birthday, so it was perhaps puzzling to see one so young by himself in the forest. They congratulated me on getting such a fat deer but I told them it was more luck than skill. The man could see by the fire light that the rest of the meat hung in the tree.

After a good night's sleep and a good meal prepared by his woman, the man told me they were also going to my home camp and would be glad to help carry the meat. I accepted the offer, not only for the help with the meat, but because my having them along as my friends would cause the men who were seeking me to think twice before bothering me.

It was a wise decision because the next day we walked right into the scoundrels. They glared at me and their fury increased when the man asked what had happened to make their equipment water-soaked and stained.

He supplied them with dry tobacco and the woman worked on their furs to dry them. They spoke not a word to me and the man knew there was something amiss. Later he was to learn of my problem with them and he and my relatives would have a great laugh about it. But I had bad enemies about me now.

5. Becoming a Man

There is a period here I would rather forget. But it is this time that changed my whole outlook on life and made me a bitter and uncaring person. The past hard times with the loss of my family, friends and village probably had already hardened me.

I was now hearing more and more about the White men, who, it was said, were building their own villages in our land. The ones nearest to us spoke a different language than the ones who had come to my village when I was a young child. They settled by the salt water, not too far from our present village. I had not made personal contact with them as yet, but the talk in our village was always about them.

I had to stay near the village now, to learn the customs of my adopted family, so I could be brought into manhood and be named. It was a lot of work and the ceremony lasted for weeks. I had to wash in the river every day and this meant walking to the river without a bit of clothing on. Nudity was a common thing for these people and every tribe.

My problem was that I was shy. The reason being that I was rather well developed in my private parts. Many of the men made sport of me. They told me I did not need a spear, just put a point on it and that is all I needed. The women of the tribe made many lewd and suggestive remarks also.

I had the unfortunate luck to run into a group of boys who were friends of the ones I had beaten up previously. They did not hit me, or allow anything that would show, like bruises or cuts. They just tied me up and staked me out on the path leading to the river. They too were naked, as I was, as they were due for their initiation soon.

It was about mid-afternoon before anyone came along and thankfully it was the girls from my tribe. They were my adopted sisters; the oldest was about eighteen, the other fourteen and the youngest was twelve. They recognized me and stood and examined me carefully, making remarks about my manhood.

I asked them repeatedly to set me free, but they just stood there and giggled. Finally the oldest untied my hands and I soon managed to free myself. I ran to the lodge and sat by myself in my furs.

During that night the oldest girl came to me and stayed until morning. I was exhausted by the time she left me. This was to happen every night from then on with either her or the next youngest girl. I finally made them both with child, or I thought so. But they denied I was the one because they had slept with many boys.

When the day arrived for my initiation and naming to manhood, I was well prepared and wanted to get it over with. The first thing the elders did was to shave my head down both sides so that only a tuft of hair remained down the centre from my forehead to the back of my neck. I was to let the hair at the back of my head grow until it hung down my back. When it reached that length I would have a bone with feathers stuck into it.

I was taken to the fire pit with the others, where we were painted by the Shaman with many magical designs and cuts were made on our faces and arms.

Into the cuts they rubbed fire ash mixed with dyes of many colour, mostly red ochre.

We were then lectured, for hours it seemed, first by a Shaman then a chief. This went on and on, interspersed with singing and dancing. We were given very little to eat all this time. When the ceremonies were over late in the night we were all herded into a lodge and put under guard to sleep and get ready for the following day's ceremonies.

In the afternoon of the last day, we did not know what was in store for us. We did know, however, that it was the last rite that we had to go through. I was a little apprehensive about this, as I still wanted to be considered a Huron. I knew the people here now thought of me as one of them, whether I liked it or not.

The Shaman and the chiefs said a few words and then grabbed my penis and placed a bone over the skin at the end. He pulled the skin tight and then with one sweep of a flint knife cut the excess skin off. I groaned as the blood gushed out and then a man took a hot brand and held it to the newly cut part and stopped off the blood. The pain was so intense I found myself holding my breath to keep from screaming.

I had successfully passed through the cutting of my upper arms and chest without a sign, but this was a little too much. I was pulled to my feet and taken to another lodge where all the other boys were. They were all in great pain, some were crying and others just groaning. I went to a dark corner and sat down holding my private parts in misery.

Later that night they brought us food but not many could eat. I drank water and other liquids that were to help the pain. It was strong medicine, because I soon feel asleep.

When I awoke the next morning many were still moaning and in great pain. I looked at myself and I was a gory mess. Those who went outside to urinate came in with more pain than before. A man came in and said if we went into the cold stream nearby to urinate while under water it would be less painful. Many of us did this and I continued to do this until it was no longer necessary. It made the pain more bearable. The man told us to avoid women for a while as it would hurt us. I did not need this advice.

Some of the boys had infections in their arms and some in their new cuts but I was one of the fortunate that did not. It took about eight days before I healed and then I had no more problem.

6. Huron Captives

It was about this time that I saw my first White man up close. He arrived one afternoon with a group of warriors from a nearby tribe. He was rather short, with a heavy cloth shirt and pants, and he wore rugged-looking shoes. The most noticeable thing about him was his face. It was almost covered with hair. He smoked a white clay pipe and had a voice that was low and guttural. He was nothing like what I could remember about the people that had come to my home village.

He seemed only interested in furs, for which he traded many beads and pieces of cloth. He was a happy person and smiled a lot. He was continually surrounded by our people and did a good bit of trading.

I could only watch in curiosity, because I had only a few skins, which I used for myself. The White man and the Indians with him stayed a day, then, as suddenly as they had appeared, they were gone. The village talked about them for many days after that. I took to the forest again and hunted almost every day with some success. I was now almost fourteen, and my foster family wanted me to have a woman. This I did not want, as I considered them a burden for which I had no need. I usually had a woman for mating any time I wanted one and the girls were still available even when married.

I wanted to return to the Huron village where my people still lived. If my immediate family was not there, perhaps one of my relatives would be, or a member of the Bear clan, which was my tribe. I knew many had left when I was there with Grandfather. They were spread throughout the area, hiding from the Iroquois. They were hiding from the people with whom I now lived, but did not consider my own people.

My opportunity came sooner than I expected. In early spring of the following year, the warriors left the village sooner than usual. About two months later they returned and to my surprise had three Huron men with them as prisoners. One man was around twenty and the others were around my age. They were badly marked up and beaten but showed much courage still. They were tied to posts in the middle of the village and were shown off in pride by the warriors. After that they were left to the women, who beat them and poked them with sharpened sticks.

This went on for two days and then it was decided by the elders that they would be tortured and killed. I was sick about this and determined to help them if the chance came. That night the torture began. The Shaman began to remove skin from the eldest of the prisoners using a sharp knife and peeling the skin off in strips. The idea, apparently, was to get the skin off without shedding any blood. Usually the victim loses a lot of moisture through this type of torture and has a terrible thirst.

In this case the victim showed great courage, not making a sound. When the Shaman stopped for the night, he was fairly well, but without skin on the front of his body. I was sick at my stomach from this and had left after they started. I did not know what I could do, but decided to try to do something during the night. I gathered together all the possessions I had that I could take with me and tried to get some sleep.

As I still made my bed at the forest edge, it was easy for me to keep an eye out for movements in the village. After I was sure that the way was clear, I went to the men tied to the posts. I entered the village on all fours, with my skin blackened with mud. I made my way slowly, taking care to make no noise and staying in the shadows of the lodges when possible.

Finally I was behind the men and, speaking softly in Huron dialect, told them to be quiet. I went to the one boy first and cut his bounds. He almost fell to the ground, but I told him to stand as he was, as though still tied. I went to the other boy and did the same for him. I then told them to go in a certain direction and I would follow them.

When I was sure they were well on their way, I examined the older man. I realized that I could not help him to escape as he was too far gone. I took up a good sized stick from the ground and hit him on the head twice, to make sure he was dead. I knew this was better than suffering anymore, but it made it no easier on me. It bothered me the rest of my days, although I was to kill many men in the future. I then hurried after the others, picking up my furs and things where I had left them earlier.

As I turned to look at the village once more, I was surprised to see my foster father looking after me. He was standing where I had released the men. He waved his arm at me as a sign that all was well. I think, to this day, that he knew me better than he let on and knew what I was going to do that night.

7. Escape

I had to run to catch up to the boys, who were still scared. They were puzzled by my appearance and found it hard to believe that I was a Huron like them. My appearance was a shame, even to me, but I intended to make them look like Mohawks to help in our escape from this country.

We went to the east, because I knew this would confuse the Mohawk, who would expect us to go to the northwest. We continued in this direction for about three days, until I was confident that we were not being pursued. The first night out, I cut the hair on both boys, so they resembled mine as close as was possible. I also took ochre and tried to stain the marks on their arms to resemble mine. This would not stand up to close scrutiny but would pass from a distance.

I could not feel safe until we were at least to the north of the great lake nearer to our homeland. We camped and traveled by night as much as possible. The boys, who were not much younger than I, soon let me do the leading as they were still feeling ill from their experiences. I was not too sympathetic with them, because I had been hardened by my own. The boys were named Fish Water and Sleeping Dog and had been brought into manhood just that summer. I wanted to get rid of them as soon as I could, but this was not to be for awhile.

I headed almost to the salt water lake before I turned north. It took about nine days before we came to the big river. We had passed within earshot and, in a few cases, eyesight, of many Iroquois camps. In one case, we had to detour around a fairly large village, just south of the river. The river here was not as wide as it was further to the south by the big lake. We just waited until dark and, taking a large log by the shore, we used it to float across the river. We entered the water and it was cold, but not running very fast. It took us about three hours to make the far shore, and we were chilled to the bone.

It was impossible to start a fire in the open by the water, so we went to the southwest, and inland for most of the night. By dawn we felt that it was safe to light a fire and warm ourselves. I learned a lot about the boys on the trail when we could talk.

They had first questioned me about my being with the Mohawk. It took a long time to relate what had happened to me, but they were eventually satisfied with my story. They told me they were taken from a small village to the west of my own village. They were Petuns, our relatives, and were from quite a large group that lived to our west. They lived in villages as we did.

As we went south, along though not on the shore of the big river, it became apparent that we were further north than we had first thought. We got our first hint of this when we came to a river flowing from the north and into the big river. I could not remember this one and after a lot of trouble, we finally got across it as we had done before.

When we reached the other side I could smell smoke in the air and we became very cautious. I scouted ahead and what I saw astonished me. I came upon a clearing and in the centre was a fortified wall surrounding a structure such as I had never seen before. It was made of logs laid one on the other to form a wall. I could see people moving about, and they were for the most part Indians.

Then I saw the White men. One was dressed in a long dress like our women wear, but made of a rough black cloth. The other men wore pants or britches, with a shirt, shoes, and stockings. They had bands around their heads. Their hair was long and they had some on their faces. I stood on a hill overlooking this for more than an hour, before I returned to the boys and told them what I had seen. They came to the hill with me and we lay in the brush observing these strange people. We had no intention of going into this place and when we did leave, we went to the north.

8. We Head for Home

We continued along the shore, being very careful to keep hidden from view. We soon realized we were on a large island. I knew that the river that was around this island came from where the Ottawas, a tribe not unfriendly to us, lived. They were related to the people who lived to the north of us and to the Algonquins. We now waited till dark and entered the river again, going to the north, or upstream. We then turned to the south shoreline and followed it for a few miles, before we made camp. Being very tired, we slept without eating.

Next morning we attempted to change our appearance again, so we did not look like Mohawk, but like our own people. Except for our hair, this was done easily. The two boys were nearly clear of the marks I had painted on them and could wear their hats to cover their lack of hair. I had to wear a jacket to cover the marks on my arms and chest, as well as a hat to cover my head.

I went ahead as usual, because I could move faster than the others through the bush and had a better chance to run away and warn them if observed. We continued upstream for more than eight days, before we decided to go west toward the setting sun.

Hopefully this direction would take us to the land of many lakes and swamps and we could get to our homes more quickly. We passed a number of camps and villages on our way, but, although we were in a friendly area, we had no intention of getting noticed by others. We were taken by surprise one morning when we walked into an ambush of several warriors. We fought with all we had but we were no match for them. They laughed at our efforts and then calmed us down by telling us they meant us no harm but were curious as to who we were and where we were going.

They took us to their camp nearby and the women cleaned our scratches and fed us. We now had to explain who we were and how we came to be in their land. It took most of the night by their firepit to explain everything and they showed much interest in my markings and story. I did not tell them that I had to dispatch one of the Mohawk prisoners.

They let us sleep past dawn in the morning and it was good to have food cooked by a woman and done so properly. We had eaten everything either raw or poorly cooked for so long. What dried food I had brought with me had long ago been used up.

After we had eaten, the boys and girls of the camp took us to the river. We had to remove our battered cloths and give them to the girls to be washed and mended. The older girls looked at us sitting by the water, until, embarrassed by their frank stares, we went into the water.

It was not long before everyone had shed their clothes and joined us. The older girls made no bones about what they wanted and before long we were in the brush by the river with them. I had met these people before. Grandfather and I had lived with one of them by the waterfall after he had lost Grandmother. The girls were not like the Mohawk, who were thinner and more agile and would make mating an athletic event. These girls were fatter and though nice, were very dull while mating.

After an hour or so, I began to lose interest in them and got into my clothes. I went to the lodges and, seeking out the mother of the other children, asked if we could go on our way the next day. She said we must ask the men that night by the firepit to get their permission. That night they told us that we must stay with them and become part of their tribe as we had no tribe of our own now. They had heard that most of our people had been wiped out by the Iroquois.

When I lay in my furs I could not sleep. I remembered that, during our talks, I had learned that they now did much trading with the White people. I learned also that they could not get enough furs to trade. I realized they needed all the people who could hunt, to do so. They only wanted us to stay so we could get more furs for them. With this in mind, I made plans to escape as soon as possible.

As with our own people, this group would set snares for beaver and muskrat. It was a daily chore to examine these traps. If you did not, other animals would come and steal your trapped animal. The other two boys and I were set to work the next morning, going separately with other men. When we knew the routes to take to cover the traps, we went alone. I soon learned to run from trap to trap and was able to estimate how long I would have to effect an escape.

I planned things very carefully with the other two boys and it was decided that I would act as a decoy and lure the men to follow me so they could escape. I told them to go in a certain direction and I would catch up to them in the following days. They were to travel by night and leave certain signs for me to follow.

9. We Escape Again

The next morning I gathered together what I owned and went out onto the trap line. After I had run through my trap line, I made my way slowly to the camp. When I was within shouting distance, I dropped the animals on the ground. I yelled to the people that I was leaving and took off into the forest with them after me. I ran hard for about two miles and then waited so they could catch sight of me resting.

I kept this up until late evening, running hard for about two or three miles and then resting. When they came in sight I would shout to get their attention and then run on again. This gave them no time to rest. After it was too dark to run further, I climbed a tall pine tree and hid myself in the branches. In the first light of morning, I waited to hear them approaching and then took off again. By this time we were about ten miles from the village and I decided that I had given the other boys enough time to get well on their way. I waited until I heard them coming close and then changed direction. I made a long circle around them, passed the village again to the south and, running at a regular pace, continued on the rest of the day. By nightfall, I was some twenty-five miles to the west of the village.

I made a light meal from dried meat and some berries and fell asleep in a ravine covered with leaves and brush. In the morning I drank at a spring and started to run again at an easy pace, watching for signs of the boys. At midday, I ate some berries and roots. I then walked along, no longer worrying about being followed, but keeping my attention on not being observed by others. I knew there were many villages and camps in the area. The White Man had made it so attractive for the people to trade that it was now the primary occupation.

The competition among the different groups was so great that I had to keep a sharp eye out for the hunters and their trap lines by the waters. I saw many traps and trails through the forest. I passed numerous camps and could see pelts spread on frames to dry.

I finally had word of the boys from a young man near the area by many lakes. He too was attending a trap line when I came upon him, and, seeing he was occupied and alone, I approached him. He was startled, but friendly, and was more than willing to share food and give directions. He also told me the ones I looked for were not more than half a day ahead of me.

He had not spoken with them but knew they had been fishing below a small waterfall, where his father had seen them. I thanked him and ran along in the direction he had shown to me and before dark found my friends setting up camp by a river. There was a small weir by the water and we helped ourselves to a few fish from it. As we were too scared to light a fire we just ate the fish raw, being so hungry we left only the scales and fins. They had seen no sign of pursuit when they escaped, because everyone was chasing me. I told them what I had done and we had a good laugh.

The next morning we wasted no time on eating, but made our way to the west as fast as we could go. Ice was forming around the edges of the ponds, so we knew we would be in for colder weather soon. We tried to pick a few berries as we went along, to stave off our hunger. By dark, we were tired, cold, and famished. We tried to get some frogs but it was now too cold, so we just ate berries. I gathered a few roots from the bulrushes and, peeling them, left them in water overnight. By morning they were soft enough to munch on, until we could find some more substantial food.

About midday, we came upon a camp with only women in it. We asked for food, but the only thing they had ready to eat was some corn mash and some greens they had gathered that morning. The corn mash was left over from the meal the evening before. They put the greens in a pot with the corn mash to make a thin soup, which we ate with relish. One woman had a piece of dried meat, which she said she had kept for emergencies. She offered it to us when she realized that we were so hungry. We took it with us when we left them, chewing on it as we walked along.

It was not usual for them to be so generous with strangers, but they could see that we were very young and would not harm them. I was sorry we had nothing to offer them in return, but made a mental note to help someone else someday.

We were now running into more familiar territory. There were open fields and old cornstalks around. We passed by some small camps near these, but they were abandoned. The people who worked these fields during the summer had returned to their main village for the winter.

10. My Ancestral Home

We now found enough to eat from people we met, who, though not our own tribe, were related. I approached my own village with some misgivings because I realized much would be changed since I had been there.

The longhouse where I had lived with my parents was in the old—or, as we called it then, the lower—village. It was at the base of the hill, near the water. It had palisades all around, with the gates facing the water and the hill to the south. The newer, or upper, village was at the top of the hill to the south. It also had palisades, but not as many as the lower village.

The lower village was the original village of my grandfather, though he had refused to live within its palisades. He had lived just out of the village, halfway up the hill toward the upper village, which had been built a year before the White Man came. His lodge was almost opposite the graveyard of the old ones. The graveyard was used in the days of the original inhabitants of our village and was considered holy ground.

The newer graveyard was at the top of the hill, just beside the new village. The people were buried here, but only temporarily. Every ten years or so, they were taken to a communal grave, as decided by the people. They always picked a spot for this large grave near a village which was being abandoned as the land had given out, or water was no longer plentiful. Sometimes many people died in a village and it was believed to be cursed, so they would move.

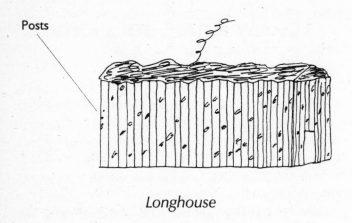

Posts

Longhouse

It had been decided many times to move our old village, but the people would not move, as it was very old and the birthplace of the Huron nation. Building the upper village had been the solution to make more room for our expanding population. This was not a big deal, as it only took us about six months to build a new village. But this did not include all the new palisades that were needed.

Grandfather's lodge was between the two villages. It backed on a stream that did not have water all year, as it dried up during the summer months. He actually had two buildings, one for storage and one for living. The lodges in the village had one large room with holes in the roof so the smoke from the firepits could escape. The areas within were divided for family groups to live in. A small room at the entrance was used for storage of food.

Dogs, field mice, and insects were the problem inside the lodge. The mice ate our food, and the dogs and kids made a lot of noise. The fleas bothered all of us. Grandfather used to keep a big fat snake in his storage area which kept the mice away from his provisions. It was not unusual, when we sometimes stayed with him overnight, to wake up and find the snake in bed with us, trying to keep warm. Grandfather was very fond of this snake, and kept him many years. He never had a dog around, although at one time my grandmother kept two baby bears. When the bears were big and getting to be dangerous, the people of the village wanted to eat them. But Grandfather and Grandmother sneaked them away to the forest at night and they were never seen again, much to the annoyance of the villagers.

The lower village palisade had a platform on the inside, to make it possible for defenders to look down on invaders, and to extinguish any fire that might have started against the walls. The palisade was usually made in an oval shape around the village. Sometimes a lookout tower was built a little higher than the posts, so as to give a guard a better chance to spot the enemy approaching. This was not always successful, as curves in the wall often afforded a hiding place for them.

We approached my village from the east and I was surprised to see that most of the upper village was gone. The palisades and most of the lodges had been burned. The few people there were mostly old. I went down the hill toward the lower village and could see that the old palisades had been replaced by new. I went in the south gate through the many twists and turns and came into the village proper. I was amazed to see that most of the old lodges were gone. They appeared to have been burned and torn down. Most of those left were down by the water's edge.

There were now about twenty lodges, where before there had been fifty or more. I went over to the buildings and looked for someone familiar. I soon found people of my tribe and they were amazed I was still alive. They had heard about Grandfather's and my capture by the Mohawk and wanted to hear my story about things since then. They made us welcome and fed us well and let us sleep in the lodge that night. The next morning I went to the spot where my grandfather's lodge had stood and all that was left was a bit of burned ash. I then went up the hill to the graveyard and was shown where my family had been hastily buried by the tribe. They had put Grandmother beside her daughter, my mother. I sat there many hours feeling very sad.

11. The Boys Arrive Home

I knew I could not stay here feeling sorry for myself, and the two boys with me were very anxious to get to their own village. We therefore left the next morning and, knowing it was only a few days to their villages, walked quickly along.

We passed many small villages along the way, mostly Huron, but eventually we started to meet the Petun people. They were surprised to see us, as it was now quite cold and we had to contend with snow.

When we came to the area of the boys' home, they would not be content, but rushed ahead, leaving me at the rear, dragging most of the luggage. By the time I arrived at the gates of their village, I could hear the noise of their arrival and it seemed the whole tribe was shouting at once. When I was inside the palisade, I just dropped everything and sat down with my back to the wall where, in all the excitement, I could stay unobserved for a while.

Everyone was running about shouting and calling each other. People were still tumbling out of their homes. I could see it was a large village, with about thirty lodges of various sizes. I surmised the population was around nine hundred people.

They were surrounding the boys and asking questions of them, which they did not give the boys time to answer. I could see that I was in for a long wait.

Eventually the cold started to get to me, so I began to look around for a warmer place. An older man came and asked me to go with him into one of the lodges, which I did without question. It was warm and as usual smoky inside, but I was happy to be there. The man gave me food, and I was soon dozing off.

I awoke when the people started to come inside the lodge again from outside. The man had put a fur over my shoulders and sat beside me. He spoke when he saw I was awake and wanted to hear my story and why I was with the boys. I told him it was their story and I preferred to have them tell it. He just laughed and said he was curious to hear why a Huron looks like a Mohawk and has their marks on his body. Are you an enemy that has deserted his tribe, or are you here to get ransom? I told him I was a Huron.

I could tell by the look in his eyes that he knew there was a story to hear and he was willing to wait. I was to learn later that this man was the Hereditary Chief of the tribe. The boys were to spend many days telling and retelling the story of their adventures. I kept my silence, until at last they wanted to hear what I was doing in the village of the Mohawk. I told everything I could about the affair and they seemed satisfied. I told all, except the family of the one I had to leave there. This was something I did not want to discuss.

It was a fortunate time, or unfortunate, depending on how one looked at it, that they were having the Feast of the Dead ceremonies the next week. It was being held in a small village, not far away, that was being abandoned.

This was the ceremony where they brought all the bones of the ones who had died during the past ten years or so into one place and buried all of them in one large grave. This was quite a long and sad ceremony and it became very boring.

We, the Huron, had the same ceremony and I had never attended one, but had heard about them from others in the tribe. My grandfather would have nothing to do with them, but he had died away from his village and my grandmother had been put into a common grave. Since the time of the older people, the tribe had not had a Feast of the Dead. This was because so many had died recently and the people were so scattered.

I went with my host more out of curiosity than anything else. People were busy up to the day we left the village, digging up their dead, to get the bones to take with them. Some who had died recently were put into hot water and their bones were scraped of all flesh and put into the sun to dry. I had seen this done before by my own people, even when they were not put into a common grave immediately. Some just did not want to bury their dead. Sometimes when it was a very young person who had died, they were buried under the floor of the lodge that their family lived in.

When we arrived at the village where the ceremony was to take place, I noticed it was deserted. As was usual, they had chosen a village that was being moved from its present location. This village was to the southeast of my own village, below a big lake. The soil was no longer productive and since there was no good soil in the area, they were moving the village about ten miles south.

They had dug a circular hole about eight feet deep and about twenty to thirty feet across. The next day, after proper ceremonies, people began to place their dead family members' bones into the hole. It was the duty of two appointed men to stay in the hole and place the bones. A small platform had been built by the edge of the hole and from there the bones were handed to the men below with great ceremony. This went on and on for days. It took over two weeks to put all the bones in the hole. Most people used the time to renew old friendships and to give and receive the latest news.

After they were finished with the burials, they filled in the hole with much wailing and crying. They put four poles over the site and on them the different tribes hung various items to commemorate the dead. The Shaman would place an animal skull, some shells, feathers, or beads on the poles and ground, to drive away bad spirits. Bowls of grain, dried berries, or perhaps the favourite food of the deceased was placed on the ground to please the dead. This was done to keep the tribe together in life and in death.

I went back to the village, as I had heard that the White Man had put up a lodge nearby. I heard also that the one in a black robe was teaching them a new religion about a man who had died to save them. I was curious about the men and wanted to see them. Apparently, if you accepted this dead man as your only God, it made it easier to trade your furs with the others.

12. My First Encounter with a Trading Post

The boy Fish Water and I did not stay around his village long. We packed some food and went on our way to the northwest. The village we were looking for was to the north on the big water and it took us three days to get there. At first sight, there was no evidence of any White man. Then I noticed a building similar to the one we had seen by the big river. It was much smaller and was within the village palisade. There were four white people; the one with the black robe was the leader.

They paid no attention to us as we stood observing. They were talking with a group who had furs to trade. They talked for some time, then one of the men went into the lodge and returned with a few small things, for which the men gave up a bundle of furs.

The boy and I went to the other side of the village, where he had relatives. They took us into their lodge for the night.

The men who had traded the furs were from this lodge, so we had a chance to see what they had traded for. They had coloured beads, white pipes, a small knife and a piece of cloth. Everyone was happy for them. I lay awake, thinking I should start the trading game to get these things also.

The next morning I spoke to Fish Water. He was more than happy to try to get enough furs to trade. It was now very cold and there was much snow, so we decided we would try the swamps and streams nearby.

We borrowed rawhide and snowshoes from the people in the camp and set out the next morning. The snow was not very deep, so two days later we were at a large swamp. We went to work as quickly as possible, setting snares in holes in the ice to get beaver, first making sure the huts were occupied. We also set snares on game trails to get fox and rabbits. We left raccoons out of our plans. It took us over three weeks to get just ten pelts, which we had scraped and rubbed with ash from our fires. We then stretched them on willow frames to dry.

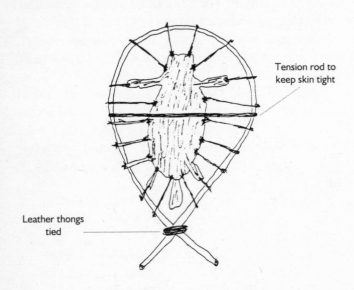

Willow branch bent to shape and tied to form drying rack for skins

We had a lean-to against a tall outcropping of granite, facing the south to get warmth from the sun. The snow kept drifting in, but this helped to conceal our camp from anyone passing by. We came across several camps and traps in our travels, but we never bothered them and hoped they would not rob ours. Sometimes we thought we had been robbed, but could not prove it.

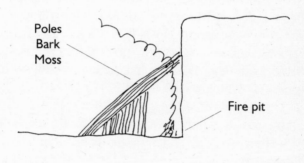

Poles
Bark
Moss

Fire pit

Lean-to

The weather got worse and some days we could not leave our camp. By the time spring started to show, we had a few furs. When the water cleared of ice, the muskrat were so plentiful that we had more than we could make frames for.

On a warm day in spring, we decided that we had enough furs to trade, so we left. The village was a scene of activity when we approached. Men were coming from the forest in every direction with their furs. We dropped our bundles at Fish Water's lodge and went to observe how the trading was going on.

There were many of our people sitting around the White Man's lodge, with bundles of furs at their feet.

The white man was negotiating with men when we arrived and they seemed to be making good deals. After watching for most of the day, we realized we were too young to negotiate with the White Man, so I asked Fish Water's father if he would do it for us. He agreed and the next day he negotiated a good deal for our furs.

But even after getting as good a deal as we had expected, there was not much left after we paid for the use of the tools and food we needed. It was then that we decided to go to my own village and work from my own people. Fish Water agreed that there were too many looking for too few furs in his area. We left the next morning, taking everything both of us owned, which wasn't much.

It took us three days to get to my village. After talking to the members of my tribe, we decided to go on further, as there were too many hunting near the village. We were able, however, to get more equipment to hunt with. We were in one place long enough to gather the things necessary for me to make our own tools.

The next morning we went in the direction that Grandfather and I had taken years ago. We traveled for many days, going over and through many swamps and rivers. When I knew we had arrived by the old camp in the place where Grandfather and I had lived with the Ojibwa woman, we stopped. There was nothing left of the camp now, as all signs had disappeared. We set up a camp for ourselves, the same as Grandfather and I had done years before.

For the first few days we just lay around doing only what was necessary. We picked some early spring berries and took fish from below the waterfall by the camp. It was good to rest awhile. Fish Water got used to the area before we began to hunt in earnest.

I knew we were in the southernmost area of another tribe, but we hoped that since I had been there before, they would not bother us.

We finally got down to business and during the next few months we worked hard and soon had a good supply of furs for trading. Up until then we had not been bothered by anyone and felt ourselves lucky to be left alone. But our fortunes changed.

13. Robbed

One evening a family group came into our camp. They were from along the river to our southeast and not related to us, but to the Algonquins. They were friendly enough and showed no hostility toward us. There were four men, a father, three sons, two daughters, and their mother. Two of the men were older than we and the others were younger. We sat by our fire pit, telling about ourselves until late. They went to their furs and we went to our lean-to. I did not sleep much, as I did not trust these people.

In the morning, the people ate a light meal and bid us goodbye. They went to the north, so we felt they intended to leave our area, but we kept to the camp all day, just in case. The next morning we went to our trap lines and when we returned that night, a lot of our furs were missing. This filled me with much anger and I knew our visitors were responsible. We immediately packed lightly and set off in pursuit.

It was soon apparent that they had not gone far from our camp, knowing we were two young people and no match for them. But Grandfather had taught me well and my experience with the Mohawk had helped to make me cautious. We observed them carefully from a distance, keeping out of their sight. We played a dangerous game, knowing they would certainly kill us if we attacked them.

By observation, we saw how they would do the

same things every day and after a week, we decided
what we would do. The next morning, we left our furs
before daylight. We made our way to a trail that we
knew two of the men followed every second morning.
Lying in some brush close to the trail, we put arrow
to bow and waited. In a short while, we heard the men
coming and, when they were just past us, jumped up
and let go our arrows, at the same time pulling our
tomahawks from our belts. My arrow hit one man in
the back and by the time he knew what was
happening, my tomahawk had crushed his skull. I
turned to the other man and he was getting up from
his knees as Fish Water was getting to him. He raised
his arm to strike, but the man grabbed him around
the waist and they both fell to the ground with the
man on top. I rushed over and hit the man and he
gasped as I hit him again.

Fish Water lay there and just stared. I knew this
was the first time he had attacked another man and I
could understand how he felt, but it was them or us.
Quickly, I pulled the two men to the river nearby and
threw them into the water, watching as the current
carried them from sight.

We both sat down by the river's edge to get our
breath back and plan what we had to do next. We
knew that the two we had killed would be missed
when they did not return as expected. We also knew
that the other men would come to see what delayed
them. We were aware of the trail the other man had
taken, so we just hid further along, closer to their
camp and waited. About six hours later, we heard the
man approach. With our bows strung, we waited. As
soon as he passed, we got up and aimed carefully. We
both shot at once. My arrow hit our quarry at left of
centre and Fish Water's hit him a little below mine,
on the opposite side.

I jumped out with my tomahawk raised, but there was no need to hit him, as he was dying. We grabbed his legs and dragged him to the river and though he groaned a little, we paid no heed. He was dead by the time we threw him into the river.

We now had only the father and the women to contend with, before we could reclaim our furs. We made a long circle around our enemies' camp and got as close as possible without being seen. The women were sitting by the firepit and the man was lying on some furs dozing. I crawled on my stomach, keeping as much brush between me and the people as possible. Just before I reached the man, one of the girls made a noise. It caught me by surprise and made me move sooner than I had wanted to.

I could only jump up and run to the man, swinging my weapon at him. It caught him on the side of the head, bouncing off, but it stunned him and he fell back unconscious. Meanwhile, Fish Water had jumped over to the fire pit and bade the women to sit still, by menacing them with bow and arrow. I quickly bound the man's arms behind his back and then went over and bound the women. They knew full well who we were and also why we were there.

We then sat all of them by the fire, where we could watch them, while we examined our furs and took what food they had ready and ate it. It was such a relief to have done what we had to do and still not be hurt. The food was welcome, as we had not eaten for two days and needed something to keep up our strength. I had Fish Water watch, while I slept a little and when I awoke after dark, he slept while I watched. The man was awake by now, and although he had a sore head, he could talk. He said he would like to live and for us to take what was ours and leave.

I told him all we wanted was our furs and that they

had suffered enough for what they had done. I released the youngest girl and made her feed them, after which I bound her again. While doing so, I could feel she was a well-built young woman and I realized that I had not been with a woman for a very long time.

After Fish Water awoke, I pulled the girl into the bush nearby and spent the rest of the night using her. This may seem an awful thing to you, but it was the accepted way in our society. Fish Water took the older girl into the bush during the day and used her. We lay about most of the day, doing nothing but watching our captives; the man seemed better as the day went on. Next morning we packed what was ours and some that wasn't and left their camp. We took the two girls with us to help carry the load of furs and other things.

The man was in no condition to follow us. After we had assured him we would release the girls, to return to him after we got to our destination, he agreed. The girls seemed willing to come with us, though we knew they did not forget that we had killed their brothers. We had to bind them at night and even when we did use them, they were not friendly to us.

The trip to our own camp was without incident and we took our time to get there. When we arrived, the girls immediately wanted to return to their family. So, with reluctance, we let them go, giving them both some furs and the shining metal we had traded for earlier. For the next few days we had to work hard going about our trap lines, for the traps were full.

About a week after our return, we decided that we should get our furs to my village and trade for things that we needed or wanted. It would be all we could do, to carry them as we now had three big bundles.

As we came closer to our own territory, we met many of my people, who told us to avoid the village, as there was a great sickness there. It appeared that the White Man had brought an illness that was strange to us and the Shaman had no way to cure it. They said many of our people had died from it and for us to stay away.

We did not know what to do, and after we had discussed our problem with many, it seemed the best plan to go to another village, which was not so badly hit. It was south of my own and not as large. The village was by a very small lake and it was said that there was a good trading post there, manned by people called the French and by a good man in a black robe.

This meant a further three days on the trail, but there was no other way to go. When we arrived, the man in the black robe questioned us carefully. He wanted to find out where we had come from, so as to be sure it was not from my own village, where the sickness was at its worst. We were then allowed inside the barricades and it was no trouble to trade our furs.

This time we traded directly with the trader ourselves, so we were able to keep what we got, except for gifts to the Shaman of the village. One thing that pleased me was that I got a knife that had a wooden handle and was very sharp. Fish Water got a fine red blanket and both of us got strings of white beads that we could trade with the women.

We stayed for a long time, and then, since the snow was coming, we spent our time gathering berries and fish for the winter's food. At first we did not plan to stay here, but with the cold weather and the warm lodge, our ambition left us. It was easier to enjoy the good life of the village. There were lots of women and food.

By the time spring came, we were broke. We had given away everything we had worked for the past year. There were no regrets on our part, as we had enjoyed ourselves, but now it was time to get working again.

We could not go back to the last place we had hunted, because too many people from the north had come down into the area. Trapping lines were getting very crowded, as everyone was now actively trading with the White Man, who showed no intention of losing his desire for furs. There were trading posts all over and every village had a place to trade. The White Man was everywhere.

We heard many stories of the villages that these people were building to the southeast, by the big river, and how they now had women of their own with them. I knew they were building some villages in the Mohawk country, because I had seen them by the big salt water. These were different White people than the ones we had in our area.

14. Smoke Eater

There happened to be a man named Smoke Eater in our village who was familiar with the area to our south. He told us he knew of a big valley where they had found beaver dams along the whole length of it. It was a hidden place that not many people knew about. He asked us if we would be interested in accompanying him on a hunting trip. As we had no firm plans, we agreed.

As soon as the weather permitted, we left the village heading south by southwest. We were close to the territory of a tribe called Neutrals, but were not quite into it. We traveled for more than a week before we reached our destination.

We were now in a very hilly section, bordering on the mountainous. The trees were very thick on the hillsides and valleys, so it was slow going, following game trails most of the way. Sometimes we had to move along streams and rivers to make any headway. Sooner than I had expected, we came upon a long, wide valley between two mountains, beautiful to see. We sat on a hilltop, just looking at the view for more than an hour.

We descended to the valley floor and in some places the trees closed out the sunlight and made it quite dark. Soon we came to a stream at the bottom and, following it, we came to many marshy places where there were signs of beaver and muskrat. There were small open fields here and there where deer grazed and in the marshes we came upon many moose with young.

When we had gone about twenty miles into the valley, we decided that we were about halfway. Here there was an open field and we made it our home. It took about ten days to put up a lodge and make a trap line. This we divided into three, so we would each have a section of our own. The valley was isolated. It was not really surprising that no one lived there, as it was impossible to make a garden anywhere.

It was soon apparent that we had a good place to get furs. The beaver were abundant and in the spring we were able to get many muskrat. Our lodge was substantial, so we knew we could survive the winter. We divided the time between the trap lines, picking berries, and gathering roots to dry for winter. The plentiful deer and moose would make it easy to get all the meat we wanted, but we had many beaver to eat, so the deer and moose were not bothered for the time being.

Smoke Eater was very good at skinning and making stretching racks, so by following his lead it was easier for us to stretch our hides and cure them. It was soon necessary for us to build a place to store our furs. We concealed a lean-to in the brush, so the furs would be safe when we were away. But so far, no one had come into our valley. When the beaver started to become scarce we went after other animals.

One animal we snared was the skunk. We would set the snare, tying it to a long pole, and when we had the skunk in it we would quietly sneak up, keeping anything handy between ourselves and the animal. When we got close enough, we would grab the pole and hold the skunk in the air so he could not spray us. We would walk this way to the river and hold the skunk under water until he drowned and was harmless. This also kept the hide in good condition. When this was not successful, the hunter would spend a few days in isolation and take many washes in the river. There were a few herbs that would help.

Mink, badger, martin, weasel, squirrel, and fox were dispatched by a blow on the head with a club. Beaver were trapped under water so they were usually drowned by the time we got to them. For muskrat, we set the trap close to shore, so they were sometimes on land and we dispatched them with a club. Raccoons were pretty smart animals and if left in the snare too long would chew a leg off and escape. Some of the other animals would do this too, but most were caught around the neck, so choked to death.

We tried to eat all the meat from the animals, but it was impossible and a lot of it went bad, or was eaten by other animals. This never was the case in the older days, before the traders came. We rendered the fat from the meat and used it with some herbs and juice from the bark of certain trees to rub into the hides to make them soft and pliable. The traders would smell the hides to make sure they were tanned properly. Some hides we just let dry and then laid them into bundles which were bound with ropes made of hides. This rope was made by cutting the deer skin into strips.

We spent considerable time preparing for winter. Meat was dried and berries collected. Nuts were harvested and stored, but we did not have corn to make meal, so it was decided that the man would take some furs to trade for corn meal. It was also decided that we needed a woman to care for us so he was to try to get one by trade or other means. The younger of us wanted a young one, but I knew Smoke Eater had something else on his mind.

15. Women Come to Our Camp

Smoke Eater was gone for almost two months and on his return had food and two women with him. It appeared that they were a mother and daughter from a nearby tribe who had lost the rest of their family to the White Man's diseases. Immediately, Fish Water took to the girl as an old friend and they seemed attracted to one another.

Smoke Eater and the woman went to their furs together that night and Fish Water and the girl to his. I was an unwanted person, so I lay under the stars alone. It was hard to get everyone going the next morning. Everyone except me wanted to stay in the furs. I made a meal and went out onto my trap line for the day. When I returned that night, it was good to have a meal ready and waiting.

Soon everything was into a routine and things went along well. About fifteen days after the mother and girl arrived, the girl took sick. For days she had a high fever and was out of her head. For three more days she remained in this state. Late one morning she died. The older woman and Fish Water were beside themselves with grief. Smoke Eater and I were helpless. After the girl had been buried we tried to return to normal, but I could see that Fish Water was saddened. He grieved for weeks, until he came down with the sickness and a high fever. After a few days he also died. It was a shock to me, as he had become like a brother and I was extremely fond of him.

After we had buried him, I knew not what to do. Smoke Eater, his woman, and I expected to get the White Man's disease and thought our days were numbered. But as sometimes happens, we escaped the sickness. Smoke Eater and I discussed what we should do with Fish Water's share of the furs. It was decided that both of us would go to his village in the spring and leave his share of furs with his family. For the time being, we would go on hunting until spring. Soon after that, the snow began to fall. That year the winter seemed very long.

It was one of those winters when the snow piled up and because it was so cold stayed on the ground until spring. Our lodge was almost covered over with snow. We had a good supply of firewood so managed to keep warm. The food that Smoke Eater had brought back with him soon disappeared, so we were forced at times to have only a meat diet. When spring finally arrived we relished the greenery we were able to gather for food.

With spring came the mosquito plague, which made our lives miserable. When they were nearly finished along came the black flies. We tried to protect ourselves but it was impossible. I coated myself in mud to try to discourage them but they always found one spot on my body that was unprotected.

There was always an insect of some sort to make life uncomfortable. A larger fly which we called a deer fly, could bite a large piece from your hide if it got the chance. These flies stayed around during the warm weather. Constantly we had to watch for ants, bees, and hornets, as they could prove to be a problem for us also.

We tried to gather the honey of some types of bees, but it was a dangerous job. We would watch a bear taking honey from a beehive in a tree. After the bear left, we would try and retrieve what he had left behind. We always got stung no matter what we did to protect ourselves.

If we wanted something sweet it was easier to tap the maple trees and make sugar of the sap. In our case we left this to the woman, who had the time for it. We were too busy with hunting the muskrat, which were plentiful at this time of year. There were a lot of furs to take care of so our trip to Fish Water's village was delayed until this was done.

16. I Leave the Valley

Eventually we were ready to go, leaving the woman at the camp to care for things. We assured her that we would return. As we went over the ridge at the end of the valley, I stopped and turned to take my last look at what had been my home for a year. Smoke Eater said nothing, but we both knew I had no intention of returning.

We had to travel slowly, as the furs were very heavy. It took us a week to get to a trading post. Since we were the first to arrive there that spring, we did exceptionally well trading my furs. Smoke Eater had left his bundles at the camp, so we only had mine and Fish Water's, which we did not trade. We left this for his family to do. After we left the post, we split his bundles between us to carry. This made it possible to make better time.

Even so, it took four weeks to get to Fish Water's home village in the Petun country. His family, though glad to see me, were very sad indeed with our news. We were obliged to stay and attend all the usual ceremonies given for him. His furs were given to his mother, who traded them at the post. She then gave much of what she got to the Shaman for talismans and other things, that, according to customs, went to help the dead.

The village looked different to me somehow, and it was not till later that I realized how many people were no longer there. It was still too early in the spring for people to go to summer camps, so I asked where the people were. I was told that half of the people of the village had died from the White Man's diseases; even the Black Robe and other White men had succumbed. It was apparent that hundreds of people had died.

This made me wonder about my own village and Smoke Eater felt the same concern for his. So we left at once and when we were close to our own territory, we parted—he to the lake south of my village and I to mine.

17. White Man's Disease

As I approached from the south, I was very surprised to see that the upper village was no longer occupied and most of the palisades were gone. It was not burned, so it was not the Iroquois that had caused it. As I came down the hill to the lower village, I could see that it was still there and occupied. I entered the gate and went past my lodge, or, I should say, that of the tribe.

As my eyes became accustomed to the dark I could see that many people lay about on the floor and bunks. There was much moaning and crying going on. I stopped a young girl who was going outside to ask what was going on and after looking at me in disbelief she answered that the White Man's disease was killing our people. I walked along in the lodge looking for familiar faces, but could see none and realized that half the people were missing.

I hurried outside, and seeing an older man asked him about the village, explaining I had not been here for over a year. He said that for the past three months the White Man's disease had killed almost half of the village. It was hard to believe, but later I was to find out that between the Iroquois and the sickness more than half the village had perished. He told me some families had not even returned from their summer camps the winter before as they had died there from the sickness.

He told me that most of the food was gone and they had not been fed properly during the winter, which made the sickness even worse. He also said that the White Man had left the village until the sickness was done, including the priest who had persuaded many of the tribe to his way of thinking. To be fair I must add that to trade and get a better deal on furs, it helped to listen to their way of thinking and accept their beliefs; this was not always necessary because of the demand for furs and their scarcity, but it did make a difference.

I went to the garden areas nearest the village and they had been picked clean. So I went further to a nearby village and found they too were short of food. I went into the swamp and gathered all the young tender shoots of the bulrushes I could carry and took them to my lodge. I did this for days on end, gathering whatever was edible growing around the village. I slept on furs out in the bush at night and would go out to the swamps as day began.

After about a month or so, people seemed to be on the mend and started to live more normal lives. They began by planting the garden near the village. A lot of time was spent burying the dead, which seemed to be a constant job.

There was a smell of death around the place that even a strong wind would not remove. I knew I could not stay here much longer because of the way I felt. No one seemed to think that they or the village would survive. I did not see one happy face all the time I spent there. The Iroquois had not attacked the village for some time, but all knew the day was not far off when we would hear from them again. I intended to be far away when this happened because I felt they had a special score to settle with me.

Before I go on, I must speak of something that was most disgusting to me. Because of the lack of food in the village some—or should I be honest and say most—of the people had turned to eating the flesh of their dead. They had eaten all the dogs and pets and had nothing more to eat. It had been the custom of some of our people to eat the enemy killed in war, but to eat one's own people was disgusting. When I found this out I was sick to my stomach but knew they had done it to survive.

My own tribe, the Bear tribe, did not indulge in this type of thing, although some had been pressured on the warpath to do so. I had never seen it in my own family, but Red Snake had told me it was done. It is a very painful thing to talk about but there it is.

18. I Leave Again

I had no idea what to do with myself now that the village was so unattractive to me. I just walked away one day not really knowing where I was going. I ended up between the two lakes to the southeast of the village. I spent a few days there fishing and talking to other people who came by as this was a very popular crossing point. Every story I heard had to do with the White Man's sickness. The Iroquois were the furthest thing from their minds.

One older man told me he had just returned from a camp to the east of us and had taken a lot of furs in the swamps nearby. He drew a map to show me where his old camp was as he felt too old to return there again. We spent days talking about the sickness and the White Man and he told me of finding many families in small camps who were either sick or already dead. It was a burden when you found this because you either tried to nurse and feed them or you had to bury them. Either way it took your time, especially when they were strangers to you, and not of your own tribe.

The easy way would be to leave them the way they were, but this was unthinkable to most of us. Even enemies would try to help, albeit reluctantly. The White Man had gone and left us to our own fate in an effort to help themselves. Many were nursed by our people but never us by them. A few of the black robes tried to help, but they could not be of any use.

I finally gathered what belongings I possessed and left the area, going in the directions described by the old man. I made good time the first three days, then one night as I approached a fork in the river I found a camp of strangers who were all ill with the White Man's sickness. The men of the camp were the worst off. Two were dead and the other three were very ill. Two older women dragged themselves around in a daze attempting to see to the others. Four other women were very sick, as well as several children.

As I approached, the women cried out in alarm, but seeing I was alone and young they went about their work, ignoring me in their pain. I observed the camp and went into the lodge and looked at the people. The two dead men were beginning to smell badly so I took them out by the forest and buried them in shallow graves under a low bank. I gave the women all the food I had left and, not waiting for daylight the next morning, went hunting.

I came across three animal traps that had beaver in them and, taking out the insides, left the skins there. When I returned to the camp the beaver went whole into the pot and I went to the swamp and pulled bulrushes to add to the pot with them. I was also lucky enough to find cress and leeks. When all were in the pot it made a good meal for the people and made their misery easier to bear.

For three days I hunted and gathered food for the camp and now some were showing more life than before. The younger people felt better sooner than the older ones. Some were able to help gather food and quickly gained their strength back. I was anxious to be on my way but could not desert them. One night on my return I found two other men there and they were the ones who owned the traps I had robbed of food. They showed no anger and were in fact happy

I had taken the meat. They had brought more meat for the people and talked with them for some time. These men were not of my tribe but they were all of the same people.

The men stayed the night with us and the next day asked me to come to their camp and get more food for the people. I could not refuse so I went with them. We took most of the day getting there and I had to spend the night with them. The next morning I left to return to the people loaded down with food.

Being loaded down as I was, I had to spend that night in the forest and made it to camp the next morning. The women had done a lot of work cleaning up the lodge and the campsite. Most of the illness had passed without any more deaths and, outside of weakness, the people were much better. The older ones were outside now and showed they would survive. The children ran about and, except for the grief for the two who had died, were happy.

19. My Cave, My Home

As most of the summer had now passed, I was more than ever anxious to get to my destination without further delay. The next morning I left the camp with much crying and thanks from the people. I followed trails leading northeast to the land of many lakes and swamps. It was well into fall of the year by the time I found the old man's cave that he had told me about. I quickly went about making it as comfortable as possible and getting food enough for the coming winter.

There was a village about two days' walk from the cave. There I found people willing to trade for dried berries and fish. I had to give up what tobacco I had for ceremonial purposes.

I laid out my traps as soon as I could and before long had furs drying and meat curing. The beaver were very plentiful and I knew the muskrat would be good in the early spring. I stayed clear of any area where there were other traps. It would not be very healthy for me to be found taking over other people's trap lines.

The days turned to weeks and months and I soon had many bundles of furs piled in the cave, which I tried to keep hidden from view. It overlooked a small swamp and was secluded in a group of large boulders back in a grove of alders. I had to squeeze in past huge rocks that towered above. The cave was below an overhang of granite and was about twenty to forty paces long and about four to five feet high. It never really was dry, but with some furs and a small fire it was warm enough. The smoke usually blinded me and I smelled of it all the time.

Many times I was followed when I went to the village nearby to trade meat and furs for food. Luckily I could still run very fast and my pursuers would give up the chase. Because I was a stranger in their area, they were not happy about my being there and they hoped to find my lodge and take my furs for themselves. They would not harm me as long as there was a chance for me to add to my furs and for them to find them. Many of my traps were robbed and I grew more careful to keep them hidden. It was only when the animals were caught that they were seen.

One morning on the trap line, I was distressed to see that many of my traps were empty and I knew someone was taking my furs. I was puzzled because I had always hidden them well and stayed away from any traveled area. I found many more traps robbed as days went by and now became angry.

Whoever was responsible was very cunning. They left no sign to follow. Nothing would help but for me to hide by a trap and see if they came again to rob it. I went one day to a stream and hid in a bush near a trap. I stayed there all day until well after dark and then went by walking in the stream in the dark to another place and cut across quickly to an area hidden by large clumps of brush. I buried myself under brush and leaves with a little mud on my skin so as to blend with the ground. I lay there until daylight had come and gone. It was two days before I heard something nearby and found out it was just animals. Then I heard a sound like a light footstep and watching closely saw a small figure carefully approaching along a beaver trail by the brush.

20. I Meet Leaf

Carefully the person walked, looking every way and not making any unnecessary noise. The beaver trail was of course filled with water and this left no sign. At the stream edge the intruder went through the water to my trap and examined it. As it was empty, I thought it was safe, but the person pulled it out and ruined it. This I could not understand. I now quickly made my move and, pulling my knife, jumped from my cover and lunged for the thief. As my limbs were stiff from lying under cover for so long I was a little slow and the person used this opportunity to seize a piece of wood lying nearby as a weapon.

I felt the blow to my head as we closed and staggered to the water's edge. My knife fell from my hand and all I could do was swing my fists wildly. The person was like a spring trap, thin and wiry and very quick. I grabbed at the hair and clothing to get a grip. The clothing came away and I was stunned to see the breasts of a woman facing me. I was so shocked that she got the advantage and swung the wood pole at my head and I went out.

I came to with a very sore head and wondered at being still alive. I could smell smoke and moving my head around slowly could see the woman by a small fire cooking some vile-smelling stuff. She came over to me and poured it over my head and I jumped up because I thought she was trying to burn my head off.

She laughed and picked up her pole again and stood over me warning me not to move unless she bid me.

I sat still, being unable to do otherwise. I looked at her and realized how embarrassing my situation was. Here was a young man defeated by a young woman. She could not be more than sixteen years old, which was about my age, though I really had no idea how old I was. She was wearing a short breech clout which was man's wear and her shirt was still on the ground nearby. She looked for all the world like a man except for her ample breasts. She even wore her hair like a man's.

She spoke to me and asked if my head felt much better. I replied that I thought it did though I had not thought about it right then, being so puzzled by her. She asked me if I would promise not to attack her again if she put down her weapon. I promised. She went away for a moment and came back with a small bag.

She took out dried fruit and gave me some. I ate silently, trying to make her out. Finally she said that she was from a small village to my south and she lived there with her grandfather and two brothers. She said she was not trying to steal animals from my traps but was destroying them to save the animals which she said were endangered because of the greed of the White Man and the Indians who trapped them.

This really amazed me and I could not immediately comprehend what she was talking about. Animals were here for me to trap and take their furs to trade. I could not even imagine what she meant. She spent the next few hours trying to get her thoughts into my head and I am afraid I knew as little as before. She told me to think about it during the night and she prepared to leave. I told her to stay by the fire with me for the night and she said by the way I looked at her she would be safer in the brush by herself.

After she had left I thought about what she had told me. It seemed to me there were plenty of animals. My traps were nearly always full. If it slowed down here I simply moved on to where they were more plentiful. I knew there were more animals being hunted as I had seen the huge piles of furs at the traders' place before they were taken away to the White Man's country. I knew brother fought brother for the best fur areas and realized many people had died for furs. I remembered that I had to hide my catch and knew I would have to be careful when I brought them out to trade. But this was the business we were in and we had to take the risks.

The next morning she appeared from the brush still looking like a man. I asked her why she wore men's clothing and cut her hair like a man's. She replied that as she lived in a lodge with only men, she dressed and acted like them. I asked her what she would do now and she replied that she intended to do as she had been doing, namely destroying traps to save the animals. I asked her if she would spare mine and she declined. I told her that given the chance I would cut her throat and she said she was aware of that, but I had given my word to do her no harm for the present, which I remembered.

She told me she knew where I had my cave and that she had followed me many times and had even slept there when I was away on the trap lines. This surprised me as I had been very careful about anyone knowing my position in these parts. She just laughed at me, knowing what I was thinking. She left after we had eaten and told me I was released from my promise after she had left. I had no intention of following her and told her so.

After she went away, I went to the stream and washed off my head. It was sore and there was a large bump and a small hole where she had hit me. I gathered my belongings and went to my cave, arriving there very late. The next morning I went out on my trap line and removed the traps as well as the animals in them. I had decided that I was finished with this place, especially now that it was known. Besides, I had a large number of furs to dispose of and this would bring me a good return.

21. We Meet Again

I put together such a large bundle of furs that I groaned under the weight of them when I picked them up. I left the others for another time. I went south by west to a large village where I knew there was a trader. It took me over a month to arrive there. I managed to get a good price for my catch, trading for coloured cloth, a good knife, and an axe. I also got some beads and a comb to give to any woman who was nice to me. They also gave me a water that, though pleasant in taste and a pretty red colour, made me dizzy and left me with a pleasant feeling.

I stayed in this village for a few days, enjoying the company and sharing the fire pits and stories of the elders. I had a woman for the first time in a long while but while doing so my mind went to the girl who had nearly caved in my skull. I left one frosty morning, going toward my cave again.

About fifty miles to the north of the village near dusk I heard loud talking and crept close to a firepit I could see from a distance. There were three Mohawk men and they had two prisoners, an old man and a boy. They were talking about killing them and taking their goods. I felt it was no business of mine and started to leave when I looked more closely at the boy and realized it was the girl who had bashed in my head. They had not realized as yet that she was a girl and so they ignored her and talked with the old man.

It came out that the old one and his grandchildren were from the Ottawa tribe and they were in their own territory. I had thought her to be Algonquin when I had met her, never realizing she could be an Ottawa. They were not a people friendly to the Huron or for that matter to the Iroquois. The Mohawk made regular raids into their territory and what I was seeing was a usual thing here.

I knew that if they found her to be a girl they would use her and I was surprised they had not noticed this when she had been bound. I withdrew a little further from the light of the fire for it would do neither me or them any good if I were caught, though I had my doubts I could help them. I wondered where her brothers were so I could get them to help.

I watched them until all had gone to their furs for the night and I slept fitfully under the brush where I was hidden. The next morning I watched again as they had their first meal.

They did not feed the prisoners, so I knew they planned to dispose of them soon. One man left the group to go to the stream close by and I followed him until he was far enough away to cause no disturbance. I waited for my chance to let fly an arrow at him and when it came I hit him just below his ear and the arrow pierced his throat. He made no sound as he sank to the ground grasping the arrow with both hands. When I got to him he made a gurgle in his throat and went limp, so I knew he was dead.

As I turned from him I heard a cry from the camp and upon returning to my lookout spot I could see they had struck the old man behind his skull, killing him instantly. I could hear the girl curse the men. There were two of the Mohawk left now, one young man and an older one who was the leader. They looked at the girl in surprise and the older man went to her and tore her clothes off, revealing to them that she was a girl.

They both exclaimed their pleasure and quickly had her spread-eagled on the ground naked. As the older man prepared to mount her, I let go an arrow that tore into his stomach and out his back. He stood for the moment, a look of surprise on his face, and then he fell backwards. I stood and taunted the other and he grabbed his weapons and took after me. I ran ahead, keeping in his sight, shouting insults at him. He had no chance to catch me but he could shoot arrows and these I had to avoid. I waited my chance to shoot and did hit him in the leg which slowed him down more.

I ran ahead, leaving plenty of trail and then circled about hoping to catch him from behind, but he was pretty smart. He waited for me to show and when I did he jumped me from behind a cluster of stones. He missed me with his tomahawk and I had a chance to hit him in the face. He swung again, hitting my upper arm, but my weapon caught him on the side of his face and tore away most of his lower jaw. I swung again, catching him on top of his head. It took some time pulling my axe from his skull, and by that time he was dead.

I sat down exhausted and looked around me, not really believing what had happened. It was very still and warm as I sat there, and when I looked at the man I had just killed flies were gathering on the blood of my victim and I felt sick. It was not until later that I found my own arm was covered with blood from a large gash where the man had hit me. I stumbled over to a stream and fell into it, trying to wash the terrible feeling I had from me. I cleaned my wound and made my way back to where the girl still lay bound on the ground.

I bent over and looked at her. I reached out and stroked her breast with my good hand and the look of pain in her eyes brought me back to earth. Reaching for my knife I cut her bonds. She sat there for a moment and then got up and went to gather her clothing. I stayed where I was, not moving.

It must have been more than an hour later when she called me and I looked up and she had made a meal for us. I just grunted and went by the brush and crawled under and fell into a deep sleep. I awoke later and felt chilled so I went over near the fire and went to sleep again beside it. The next morning I found myself under a fur robe and somehow my arm had a dressing of dried moss on it. I looked about and realized it was near noon, so I knew I had slept late.

There was a sound and I looked over to see the girl come from the brush carrying a bag which she opened and offered me food. I ate well because I was hungry, not having eaten since the previous morning.

I looked about and could see that the girl had buried her grandfather at the edge of the camp. The dead enemy had been dragged to the edge of the clearing and left there. I went over there and placed him near a shallow bank, pulling the earth over him after making sure he was facing downward as an insult to the enemy.

We returned to the other I had killed and with the girl's help managed to bury him in a like manner. That evening I sat with the girl by the firepit, neither of us saying anything. She just looked at me in a funny way. After about an hour she broke the silence by asking why I had intervened and saved her. I told her I did not kill for the fun of it, but that it had been necessary to save her and the reason was beyond me. I told her that I felt that she had helped me in some way, so she had caused the feeling.

She told me her brothers were back at the village where they had lived with her grandfather. They would mourn her grandfather for he was loved by them and by their village, which was beside a great river to our north. They were part of a larger group known to us as the Ottawas. We Hurons had found them to be friendly for the most part, but some could be very hostile and would charge us large fees to cross their land. We had fought small battles with these Ottawas in the past, but it had never spread to an all-out war. They were good friends with the Algonquins, who were related to them. The Algonquins were very good friends of ours. They had traded with us and had even intermarried with us.

The girl told me her name was Morning. Her tribe thought morning was about the best of times because it brought the renewal of life after a rest and renewal of the spirit, so her name was an honourable one and had been well used to name girls in her village. To make each one individual they added another name to match their time of birth. Usually it was something more noticeable at that time than others. As she was born in the spring, her second name was New Leaves. They shortened this to Leaf as a nickname, but in her language it was a short name and pretty.

I told her my name was Three Fingers at my young days and how I got it and she found this very amusing. I told her about myself and what I had done since Grandfather had died. She was especially interested in my Mohawk experiences and asked to see the markings on my arms and chest and what they meant. I told her then that I was returning to my cave to get the rest of my furs to trade off before someone else found them. She was silent for a long time, then told me she would like to accompany me even if she did not agree with fur taking. I was surprised at this and could only agree because she had somehow become important to me.

We both retired to our own furs by the fire and slept well because we had a few days' traveling to reach my cave. I tried to think about what I was to do about her and why she wanted to be with me. She was a very smart woman and this made me a little apprehensive about her.

The next morning when I awoke I found the camp had been packed and food made ready and soon we were on the trail. My arm hurt considerably and I knew she was still very sad about her grandfather, and I said many things that I hoped gave her comfort. I was rather awkward about this, as being gentle was not my usual way. We walked for the rest of the day following a well-marked trail between two lakes. On the third day we came to my cave and found all as I had left it.

On the trail, Leaf had told me she had been married at a young age to a man much older than she. Her father had given her to this man at an early age as was the custom of her people. Both her father and her man had been killed by others on the big river. They had been fighting over territory because of the fur trade. That was why she and her family did not like the fur trade, not the matter of destroying the animals for fur. After her man had died she had left her village because she could not accept being the other woman in her sister-in-law's lodge.

We packed my remaining furs into tight bundles at her instructions for she knew better than I. She was wiry and strong and was a great help to me.

We packed the food we would need and the next morning at daylight we set out, going back the way we had come a few days before. We could only travel slowly because of the weight of the furs.

That night we slept in the same furs and she was a very good partner. We made plans to stay together and would, if her brothers agreed, make it legal with the ceremonies of her tribe. If they did not agree we would be as man and woman anyway. This only meant that we would not be able to live in or near her village or mine. This didn't bother me as much as it appeared to bother her.

We eventually reached the trading station and traded our furs for useful things, mostly cloth for Leaf and tools for me. One thing we got was a big colourful blanket that we both treasured during our days together. All my furs for trading were gone and it seemed to me that my work for the past was worth it all. We spent a few days here by the trading post trying to make future plans or to agree on some. Leaf was all for making a trip to her village before winter came, but I wanted to see my own.

22. We Go to Leaf's Homeland

In the end it was agreed we would go to her village to get her family's permission to live as man and wife. Packing everything we had, we left one morning, heading toward the big river to the east. The trail to her village went just north of an area of many lakes and swamps, so we tried to avoid these by going still further north. As it was early summer, we made good time, stopping in small family camps when we could.

As was usual we traded with these people, mostly for food. There was not much time to hunt for food when traveling. It was only possible to pick some berries on the way.

After a month's traveling, we came into her tribe's vicinity and it was not long before there were people meeting us on the trail. When we entered her village many people stared at me, as I was bare to the waist and the Mohawk markings on my arms and chest were visible.

When we came to the lodge of her brothers they met us at the doorway and greeted her, but ignored me. I went and sat under a tree just outside the palisade which surrounded the village while Leaf went into the lodge to speak with her family.

About two hours later a young boy came and bid me follow him into the lodge. Leaf's family were seated in a circle and I was asked to join it. They questioned me for about four hours and then sent me out again. I sat under the same tree and slept there that night without any word from Leaf.

About daybreak I was awakened by two older men who told me that I was to leave immediately if I valued my life and that there was no way that I could have Leaf as my woman. I packed what I had with me and went into the forest, carefully looking around to see if I was being followed. I could see that the two men had been joined by another two and they were keeping me in sight to make sure I had left.

I walked away, being careful not to raise any suspicion that I had any other intentions. When I dropped into a ravine I turned quickly to my right and ran as fast as I could with the load I was carrying.

When they reached the ravine they raised a shout and took after me. I kept out of sight and made a left turn away from the village and ran until after it was dark. Carefully hiding my belongings and covering myself with dust from the trail, I ran back toward the village.

I came around by the river side and carefully crawled along its bank until I was where the women came to get water. I waited until daybreak and soon women came with their bowls to get water. I watched from the brush until one was alone and then grabbed her before she could cry out.

I quickly bound her mouth so she could not make a noise, then removed her robe and tied her securely. Putting on the robe, I picked up the bowl and went into the village. I walked quickly to Leaf's lodge and entered. The place was quite dark and they were still sleeping. I went to Leaf and found her bound. I cut the leather and motioned for her to follow me. We had not quite made it when an old man sounded an alarm. I grabbed Leaf's hand and ran for the river.

At the water's edge I pulled Leaf into the water with me and we swam to the far shore. I could hear others swimming behind us. Leaf's leather robe was now heavy with water, so I pulled it off as well as the one I was wearing. I pulled her along with me until we reached the other bank. I got up to it and then someone grabbed and held Leaf. I kicked out with my foot, catching the pursuer in the face, and he fell back into the water. Others on the far shore were pointing arrows at us but were afraid of hitting Leaf so held off shooting.

We started into the bush, Leaf holding my arm. Now the two of us were as naked as the day we were born. We ran quickly down a trail with many behind us. Soon Leaf was without breath and I knew she could not keep up with me. I came to a slight ravine and made her lie in it and covered her with leaves.

I then ran toward the pursuers until they came in sight and led them away from where Leaf was hidden. This time they chased me even further than before, well past where my belongings were hidden. Finally they tired and gave up the chase. I could hear them arguing about whether to stay where they were and continue tomorrow or go back to the village. Two decided to stay and the rest left for home.

I waited until all was quiet and very carefully made my way back to where my belongings were hidden. Taking them with me, I went on to where Leaf was hidden. As I did not have women's clothes with me she put on mine, looking for all the world like a man. We ate some dried berries and meat so as not to make a fire which would be seen. We went into our furs for a light rest before daylight.

I awoke suddenly at a noise nearby and by early light could make out a form close by. I reached for my knife but Leaf's hand touched mine and I hesitated. I looked up at the figure over me and he smiled and made a sign of peace and turned and left us.

When he had left Leaf made a sign for silence and we carefully gathered our stuff and left. About three hours later she was able to tell me that the area was full of her family's friends and her brother was the one who found us. Fortunately he was sympathetic to us and kept his silence. I was glad he felt that way as he could have done me in.

We now turned north and followed the river up into an area that was familiar to me. It was getting cooler and we had to make good time to get to my village. We managed to pick up a few pieces of clothing for Leaf, unknown to their former owners. But as the days passed by it became obvious that we needed many more clothes, as the weather was now bitterly cold. Although it was still not snowing, the cold cut into us severely.

About this time we were fortunate to come upon a summer camp that had been raided by other Indians. The people had died long ago, but the clothes were there and we took them for ourselves. It was a big help. The shoes on the bones of the dead people came in handy especially, as the snow would begin before long.

We buried the people and burned the rest of the camp before we left. The animals had taken care of a lot of things before we arrived. Nearly all the skins had been chewed by small animals so had holes in them. Leaf tried to repair these as well as she could. But it was all we had, so we were grateful. It saved our lives, I am sure.

23. We Go to My Homeland

We were now heading to the southwest, and soon the snow came. I tried to make snowshoes and managed after a fashion to provide us with some. Although they were not good, they were useful. Our supply of food was getting low and we were not able to get more in the snow. I broke the ice on the swamp to get young bulrush shoots every day, and I think they helped to save us. I found some cranberries in the swamp one day; though bitter, they were sustaining.

It was still a month before we could reach my village, and I was not sure we could make it. My clothes were in shreds and Leaf's were not much better, although I made sure she stayed wrapped in the furs all the time. I made a lean-to every night, but, although it kept the snow off, it did not keep out the cold. Twice we burned down the lean-to by keeping the fire too close and too big.

I managed to kill some small animals which, supplemented by roots and bark, made us a meal. We ate only at night as food was so limited. I was very thin and Leaf was no better. At night wrapped together for shared warmth, I could feel her bones against me and she said the same of me. Once we came upon a family by a waterfall spearing fish through the ice-clear pond below. They had a few small fish and shared with us. We did not cook them but ate them raw. We spent two days with these people by the waterfall and we ate many fish. When we left they gave us a few to take with us.

Leaf took the chance to repair some of our clothes so it was not a wasted two days. All of our goods had been left behind at Leaf's village, and it was most difficult trying to do things without tools or weapons. I had made a stout club from a piece of branch that had a hard knot on one end. With this I managed to kill some animals such as porcupines that move rather slowly.

The snow was deeper now and it seemed our feet were wet all the time. We had only shallow moccasins. We tried to stay in animal trails as much as possible and sometimes we could walk in the tracks of other people. We were now meeting more people, usually in small villages by streams.

As we turned south by the large water near my village, we came upon more people who would not help us much. The snow was now so deep that it was sometimes easier to walk on the frozen water than inland. At times the wind was so bad that it was not possible to make any distance.

We passed near where Grandfather and I had lived for a while, and we made our way there to wait out the storms. It was not possible to see any distance ahead with the snow blowing so hard. When we were near the place, I was guided by the noise of the waterfall.

I quickly built a lean-to against the granite wall and had a fire going to warm us. We huddled together in our furs to keep warm. The wind screamed about us, and the snow fell about our lean-to and drifted into high mounds in front of us.

It was two days before we could move out of our shelter. But one morning I looked out over the drifted snow and could see the sun shining. We had eaten what dried food we had, so it was necessary to look for something to eat.

Leaving Leaf in the shelter, I went to the waterfall and the open water below it and after several tries managed to spear a few small fish. As before, we ate them raw. Later I heard a noise toward the waterfall and went to see what it was and found a man and boy spearing fish.

I spoke with the man and he told me he was camped a short distance above the falls with his and another man's families. He was looking at my ragged furs and I knew he was wondering about me. He was of the Algonquin tongue so I knew he was of Leaf's people but could not know of us because they were such a widespread tribe.

I told him as much of my story as was necessary and he was sympathetic. He told me to join him at his camp and sent the boy with me to show us the way. I quickly got Leaf and what we possessed together and went to his camp.

The women were glad to see Leaf and the men were most friendly. We had a very large meal and a good talk around the firepit. I told them my story and how I had met Leaf and our journey here. They told me they were on their way north to their camp or village and had stopped here because of the storm.

When we finally went to our furs it was late and getting up at daylight was a problem, especially after such a good meal. It was hard to adjust our eyes because the snow was so bright from the sun. We stayed with these people for five days, giving me time to repair and replace our snow shoes and for Leaf to repair our furs. The women gave her enough pieces of fur to make leggings for us which would help to keep the snow out of our moccasins.

With the fish I managed to spear and some dried food supplied to us, we left for my village. It took us a further fifteen days to reach it and a great surprise was in store for me. As we approached the village I could see that most of the palisade posts were missing. And where there had been a big cluster of longhouses there were only two or three, one in such bad shape as to be unusable.

The few people remaining in the village greeted us with no enthusiasm and looked for all the world like people without life. They had a dull, painful look in their eyes and no ambition to do anything. Although they were not starving, they looked underfed.

The old ones told me by the firepit that night that they were subject to constant raids and the children were being taken by the raiders. They did not appear able to defend themselves, as most were old men. There were no children under seven in the village.

They had to hide everything; otherwise, it was soon stolen by raiders. Most of the people had taken refuge in other villages nearby. Some had gone further to distant tribes to seek safety. Many had died from the White Man's disease and some by raiders. I could see that the village was doomed. Nearly everything of value had been taken.

I had no intentions of staying around to be killed. It would be safe here until spring, but I would leave soon after. I kept busy making tools and weapons from any scraps I could find. Much was given to me by the older men. I soon had a sufficient supply of snares made and with the help of some of the old men had them set for rabbits, whose tracks were plentiful.

Before long we had rabbits to eat and fur for our warmth. This was no mean task, as there were some hundred and fifty people to feed. Having food and someone young around seemed to rouse the old people to do more. They were soon out gathering roots and bark to help feed us. The snow was deep, but they struggled about doing what they could. Everything went into a huge pot and everyone shared what we had. It kept me busy gathering the rabbits and though we longed for something different they were the easiest to trap because of their numbers. When we did get a few beaver or muskrat they went right into the pot with the rabbits so you couldn't really tell the difference.

The White men now had a station not far from the village to our west, near other people of our tribe. There were traders there all year round and they had built a very substantial lodge.

The man who was the same as our Shaman wore a cloak, so he was sometimes called Long Coat, but mostly he was called Black Coat. He had two or three others with him who did the actual trading.

Furs were traded all year and now they would take some food items in trade also. As we had nothing to trade, we never went to the post, but sometimes one of the men would come to the village in the company of our Indian friends. They would enquire as to our own hunting and would offer things for furs if we would go out and hunt them.

What we possessed we needed for our own warmth and food. There was still a lot of sickness in the village. Some people would cough at the least movement and would bring up blood. Others just went on coughing until they were too weak to move. When this happened you knew they would soon die. The old Shaman did what he could with medicines and herbs, but could not rid the people of sickness and fever.

Leaf and I built a small lodge away from the main village for our own protection as it was not impossible for some war party to attack the village even in winter. This had not happened but it could. There were no rules or honour among us now that the White Man with his fur trade and the disease had come among us.

Almost all tribal order and rules had disappeared. It was everyone for himself. Even close families sometimes broke up in anger. There was always fighting and squabbles among us. We had no defense against any organized group. Three quarters of my village were gone, mostly by the White Man's diseases. More people were leaving the village each day to join up with others around us for their own protection. Nothing of note remained of the village of my childhood. There was not one close relative to be found there.

24. We Head South

Leaf and I left just before the last snow had disappeared. We went south by southeast around the big water and into the marshes below. Here the muskrat were thickest and the birds would soon be back. They meant food for us. I made a camp on a small rise overlooking the marsh and soon we had traps set on the traveled part of the waterways. Leaf helped to set the traps and gathered the new shoots of the bulrushes to add to the pot with any meat we could get.

Every day there were muskrat to skin and put into drying frames. Leaf and I were busy from dawn to dark working the traps. In the meantime marsh birds started to arrive for their spring nesting and soon we had birds and eggs to eat. The weather seemed to get warmer every day and Leaf and I would lie on the warm ground and relax. But before long the insects came and made our lives miserable.

We stayed here for about eight weeks and collected a good supply of muskrat and a few beaver furs. Bundling all the furs and whatever else we had together, we broke camp. It took us two weeks to get to the trading post nearest us.

It appeared muskrat were plentiful that spring, so the trading was a little meagre. I got a small new axe and a knife and Leaf took cloth and needles of metal. Then we left to go further south than we had been.

On the trail we met many others loaded down with fur bundles heading back the way we had come. In our talk with them, we learned that the White people were coming into the area with large canoes made especially to carry huge piles of furs. Many were now seen at the big lake to our south.

Leaf and I continued on to the big lake. At a small village at the mouth of a large river we stayed, talking with the inhabitants and hearing stories of the White people. They told us that the large trading post was about a day's trip to the east of us on the shore of the big lake where three rivers had formed a large swampy area. The traders had built a few lodges and a large covered building with an open wall toward the lake where they stored the furs and did the trading. This place was built on poles to raise it above the ground, as were our lodges. We knew this place to be where one could disappear below the white sand.

25. The Trading Post

The trail to the post ran along the shore of the lake, and we knew if we stayed on it and did not venture inland we would be safe. Next morning Leaf and I went to the east and by nightfall had arrived in sight of the trading post. Many were gathered about trading or just watching. A short, fat, White man dressed in a white shirt and grey pants with boots to his knees was in charge of trading.

What did strike me was he wore something on his eyes made of a metal frame that had something clear like ice in it. You could not imagine the shock to Leaf and me of such a thing. You must realize we had no idea of their use and had never seen glass before. This was all explained to us later by other Indians.

The man had an easy laugh and the people trusted him. The post had many more trade goods than any of the others we had been to. A large canoe was pulled up on shore along with smaller ones to take the furs away. The White people with the canoes wore very colourful clothes and were all young.

I was told that many had White women with them at the post or where their villages were. We did not see any there. I had never seen one, but Leaf had. Many years before, when she was young, she had visited a village with her family and several of the white women had been there. She said they looked just like the White men but wore different clothes.

After the trading was finished for the day, they began to load the canoes and when this was done they left the post for the large village of the White men where the big ships waited. As each canoe was filled, they hired Indians to paddle them and paid them in trade goods. They had so many full canoes that there were not enough Indians to paddle them, so Leaf and I took on the job. Each of us had a canoe along with a White man who also had a canoe. The three of us followed the others along the shore of the lake, not trying to make time but going slowly.

At night we made camp on the shore, usually with some of the other people. A White man was supposed to be with every so many Indians, but in our case there were only the three of us. The White man was friendly, and he and I became friends. We would spend many hours talking in front of the firepit with Leaf asleep in her furs. He told me he had a White woman at the big village but had not seen her for more than half a year. He asked why Leaf and I had no children and I told him that for some reason Leaf was barren.

For days we paddled and every night the White man and I would talk. I told him the story of my life and Leaf's. He told me he was from a place called France and that his family were farmers, which made me no wiser. He described the animals they had on this farm and I could not believe him. It was not until we arrived at the village and I finally saw these animals with my own eyes that I came to believe him.

As we traveled along the shore we met many people we had not seen before. They wanted to trade with us but we had no trade goods, just the furs we were taking to the large village. Most of the time we were with other people at night, but there were many times we were at a lonely camp. It was during one of these times that Leaf and I were mating or, as you would say, making love, that the white man saw us. To us this was no great thing as we did not look for privacy as the White people did.

After this I noticed he looked at Leaf in a certain way and I knew what his thoughts were. I mentioned this to Leaf and she laughed and said she had noticed this also and was pleased and flattered. It was not long after this that one night Leaf had gone to her fur by the fireside and the man and I talked as usual. He kept looking over at Leaf who was lying on her furs uncovered to the waist.

He asked me outright if he could have her because he knew we were not man and wife but were just together without the rites of our tribes. I told him it was up to her as I was not her man. He asked me to speak with her the next day to which I agreed. It was our custom to allow visitors to have our women if they were without them. It was not a great thing with us and our women did not object in any way, but with a White man it might be different with Leaf.

So it came about the next night he went to her furs. I was watching from the shadows and I could see that Leaf was troubled because the White man wanted to lie on top of her. The Indian way was for the man to kneel down and the woman squatted over him. In this way we faced one another and the woman had control. We caressed one another first and then after the man was inserted we would caress again. The White man took a long time caressing and then after he was inserted did no more caressing. He also had control, being on top.

He was on and off her all night and I was afraid Leaf would be hurt, but the next morning she was cheerful and told me later that though it was strange she had enjoyed the experience. It turned out that she never had a quiet night after that. The White man and I took turns alternate nights, and I tried the White man's way and though strange at first gave me more insertion than before.

26. The White Man's Village

The snow was starting by the time we got to the White Man's village. Leaf and I were surprised at the size of the place and at the big wooden walk they had built over the water. We also marvelled at the huge canoes with the cloth that made them move. There were Whites and Indians everywhere and the smell and the noise was terrible. We pulled the canoes up on the beach and Leaf and I were given trade goods in pay. We walked to the large gate that guarded the village.

The palisade around the village was made of posts eight to ten feet high, sharpened on one end. They were driven into the ground close together, in a large square, and had small buildings on the corners that were higher than the walls. From here guards looked out. There were guard houses each side of the big gate, too. It was a very large enclosure and different from the type we built. Ours were never square and were made of lighter posts. We had a platform inside to stand on to fire down on anyone attacking us. Our gate was usually an offset wall that would slow down anyone, and it could be blocked.

Inside we were surprised by the buildings. They were smaller than our longhouses, but the logs were laid on their sides instead of standing upright. They also had openings in the walls. There were many of these buildings and some large ones were used for storage. It was here that I saw my first White woman. She had a full dress that dragged on the ground and she wore a hat tied to her head by a piece of cloth under her chin. Her face was so white it gleamed in the sun.

I could also see some White children, both boys and girls. They were dressed like the older ones but wore no shoes. There were also the usual men with black robes and there were soldiers around. There was a very strong odour from the white people and their cooking smelled like burnt flesh.

After a few minutes we were asked to leave the village and we went outside the palisade to the place where most of the Indians had set up camp. There were a great many different tribes, some I had never heard of before. Leaf met some of her own people and was welcomed into their camp. There was a small group of Hurons there and I went to their camp.

Not far from us was a large group of Iroquois who kept by themselves, away from the rest. The next morning the Huron left and I sat by the river thinking about my future.

A Mohawk who knew me shouted my Mohawk name which was also my secret name, and I recognized him as being one of the boys that came into manhood with me. He seemed delighted to see me and wanted me to come to his camp. I reminded him of the way I had left the village years before, but he assured me that he and the others had no bad feelings and that they understood why I had done what I did and would not expect me to do otherwise.

I went to the camp and all were happy to see me and wanted to know all that had happened to me.

I did not expect this and was happy they carried no bad feelings for me. But they pointed to the tattoos on my arms and chest and said I was a Mohawk and nothing could change this. I felt a strange feeling within me to be with my Grandmother's people. I understood this because in our culture all lineage came through the women of the tribes. It was also a good feeling to be part of a group again.

I stayed with these people for three days and then one morning I looked for Leaf and found her in the village of the White people. She had decided to go back to her own people, but first she had accepted a job with one of the White families for the winter. I left her with some sorrow and went back to the camp.

27. I Work for the White Man

On my arrival, I was told the White man who had been with us in the canoes that brought us here was looking for me. The next morning I sought him out. He asked me to work with him on his farm for the winter months and also do some trapping together in the spring on his land. I was curious about this farm which he had told me about, so I agreed. We left the next morning because it was a two-day walk to his place. We arrived there without any problems. His home was in a wooded glade surrounded by open fields. His woman and two children were happy to see him come home.

His woman was short and had long black hair. The children were a young boy and a younger girl. The lodge they lived in was a one-room log building with the logs laid on top of one another. There was a big firepit in the middle with a hole in the roof, the same as we had in our longhouses. The big difference was that they had a table, chairs, and windows and doors that closed. The windows had a cover that opened in on leather straps. There were two doors opposite each other.

The floor was made of packed earth. The firepit was made of and surrounded by stones. It had a flat roof made of wood strips covered with sod. It sloped to the back. The wood strips were made by splitting cedar logs with a steel axe. They were then laid on supporting poles.

On one end of the building was a lean-to with a door into the lodge. They kept the animals in there in the winter time. They had two cattle and two horses with some chickens and geese. None of these animals had I seen before and it took me a while to get used to them.

The family slept on bunks along the walls. I was given a place in the lean-to with the animals. At first I was nervous about these creatures, but soon became used to them. The horses did not belong to this family but to someone else who was considered most important. He just kept them for this person. During the winter they always had a big log burning in the firepit. When it burned out they would have the cattle pull another in through the door at the end and then would leave by the opposite door.

The lean-to was always warmer than the lodge because of the animals. Many extremely cold nights the family would come from the lodge and sleep in the manure piles to keep warm. The manure gave off a lot of heat. I would sit between the two cattle to keep warm. I went out every day to get meat for the table while the man repaired or made leather things for the animals.

In the spring the man and I went out and set traplines and we got many muskrat and a few beaver and raccoons. When we had many bundles we loaded them on the horses and went to the big village. He made the trades and did better than I had ever been able to do. But when he gave me my share, it was less than a quarter of what he had traded for.

This made me angry, as I had been given to understand that we were to split evenly. But he said I must pay for living with him and eating his food. I kept my silence to wait for my opportunity to get my share. I looked for the Mohawk but they had left. Later I was to learn that it was because the White men here were angry at the White men who lived in the Mohawk territory.

I stayed with the White man hoping in time to get what was mine. We started to burn over the land, and then used the oxen to pull out the stumps left in the field. I was swinging the axe from morning till night, weeks on end. My hands grew blistered and my shoulders ached all the time. I could not see doing this for food and a place to sleep and started to plan my leaving. It took place sooner than expected.

One day I was walking by the stream beside the clearing and came upon the man and his family in swimming. I sat under a tree watching them. The woman left the water and walked toward me. She saw me all of a sudden and started to scream. The man came over and told me to leave. I could not understand this but left anyway.

Later he told me never to be near where they swam again. He explained that his woman was very modest. I asked him why I could not have her as he had shared mine and he said it was not their way. If this were so, why had he used my woman?

It had not entered my mind before to want this woman, but thinking about it made me want her. She was a little on the heavy side with big breasts and heavy legs. She didn't look any different than most Indian women except for her skin colour. I had my chance very soon.

The man and I were planting as well as clearing the land. He built a small dam in order to hold the water back for watering the gardens when the rain was slow in coming.

One morning he had to take the horses to the important man who owned them and left before daybreak. I was to continue clearing by the creek.

When I got to the creek there were tracks of a deer on the bank and I could see they were new tracks. Nothing would do but that I had to follow them. This I did for the morning. It managed to stay out of my reach, so I returned to the creek area where I was supposed to have been at work clearing. The man was there and was very angry with me for not being on the job.

He swore and cursed at me and when I told him what I had been doing he just got angrier. I turned to leave, for I knew I was getting angry myself and he grabbed my arm and spun me around. His hand came out and I felt him strike me on the side of my head. I raised my arms to defend myself and he struck me again.

This time I struck back, getting him flush on the nose. Blood gushed over his face and he turned and ran to the axe and picked it up, coming at me ready to swing. I turned and ran to where I knew there were some stout poles and, picking one up, I turned to fend him off.

He rushed at me and I side-stepped in time as the axe went right by my head. He came at me again and I poked the pole at him and struck him in the forehead. He fell backward and I struck him on top of his head with the pole as hard as I could swing. He did not move again and when I cautiously approached him I could see that his eyes were almost out of his head because his skull was crushed.

I sat down to think about what had happened. I knew that the White Man would not want to listen to my side of the argument and I would be a dead Indian if they caught me. I decided I would take what was rightfully mine and head for the Mohawk country where I would be safe.

When I got to the lodge his children were playing in a field nearby. His woman was washing clothes by the rear of the building and hanging them on a line between two trees. I went into the lodge and, getting a bag, started to gather what was mine. I took out the things that I considered to be my fair share of our labours.

The woman came in and asked me what I was doing. Making no mention of her husband, I told her I was leaving. She said I had no right to take the things belonging to her and her man. I told her I had worked for them. She picked up a piece of wood and swung at me and I grabbed her and threw her on the floor.

I could feel her beneath me, and it came to me that this woman was owed to me, so, holding my knife at her throat, I pulled off her clothes. She knew I would kill her if she made a sound and though she was scared, she was concerned about her children, so she offered no resistance.

I laid on her and pushed myself deeply into her and the only sound she made was a groan. After I was satisfied, I lay beside her and tried to talk with her. I told her that her man had done the same thing to my woman and she said she did not believe this as her man was a Christian man. I hated to tell her the things I had seen the men with black robes do with our women.

28. I Leave in a Hurry

I had no need to argue with the woman, so I quickly gathered what I considered to be mine and left. I went to the south, following the river. I knew I would come to the village of the White Man that was situated on an island where two rivers met.

I did not know how long it would take for the White Man to start hunting for me, but I knew he would. It was not considered an important event to kill an Indian, but it was considered a crime to kill a White man. The fact that I had forced the White woman to mate with me was also certain to anger them. I had heard stories of what happened to an Indian who did this. I found this hard to understand. The White Man did this all the time to our women, yet suffered no consequences because of it.

In two days I was at the White Man's village and was surprised to see how large it had become in such a short time. They had erected more buildings and enlarged the palisades. The Indians had set up camps surrounding the village and many worked for the White Man. There were more people working with the wood from the nearby forest making furniture and tools. There was a trading post here where the Indian could get things by working for the White Man.

There was a Mohawk village nearby, so I went there for safety. I was surprised to see so few men here, and all were under the influence of a drink that they had traded from the White Man for furs. I had tried to drink this water from a bottle, but I did not like the taste, or the burning in my throat. I certainly did not like the sick feeling I had the next day.

I stayed here overnight. The next morning I went to the village where I knew Leaf had relatives. I was told she had left two days before with a relative to return to her home village. That afternoon I left, hoping to catch up to her before she reached her village.

Using a well-used trail, I followed the river going north. I walked until late that day and was on the trail again before daybreak the following day. I walked quickly, making good time. Around midday on the third day, while I was walking along I smelled a wood fire nearby. Turning inland about five hundred feet, I came to a small meadow. I could see a smouldering firepit and what looked to me like a bundle lying nearby.

I approached the bundle. It was then that I realized it was a young man lying there. He was dead. His head had been crushed by a blow. Looking around, I could see another figure near the trees. I approached this figure and realized it was Leaf. She had been trying to reach the shelter of the bush. I went to her, picked her up, and carried her to a small stream that was nearby.

Leaf had no clothes on and was scratched and bruised. I began washing her face. She looked at me and cried my name, then, clinging to me, sobbed out her story. She and her friend were just getting ready to leave the camp the day before, when they were attacked by two French traders. They had killed her companion and raped and beat her. Later, I helped her find some clothes and made her a hot meal.

She was still sore from the beating she had suffered, so while she slept, I buried her friend. The next morning, I told her I would look for the French people and deal with them. She said she would not want me to kill them and made me promise not to do this. I agreed I would not. I told her to make her way to the river when she felt strong enough, and wait for my return.

I left immediately, returning to the river. I found where they had beached their canoe. I knew that they had been going upstream because I had not passed anyone when I was on my way here. I left, going up the trail, hoping to soon catch up to them. I knew they had to paddle against the river current and make a few portages around rapids.

They would not think anyone would pursue them, so I kept a steady pace. Eventually I could see them as they camped about a hundred yards ahead of me. I decided to wait until morning before making my move. I slept well during the night and before daybreak went to their camp.

I crept as close as I dared to and could see the two figures beside their firepit. I carefully looked around and could see their rifles leaning against a nearby tree. They lay sleeping on the ground. I silently crept to the tree, took the rifles, and returned to the tree on the opposite side of the fire pit. I could watch them from there.

After daybreak, one man got up and walked to the edge of the clearing to relieve himself. He returned to the firepit and threw more wood on it. He did not notice me even though I was in plain sight of him. The other man groaned and got out of his bed. He too went to the edge of the clearing and relieved himself.

It was while he was returning that, with a start, he noticed me. He reached for his rifle, but saw that I had them. The other man realized what was going on and cursed. I pointed their rifles at them and told them to be careful.

All I wanted was an excuse to kill them. I told them they were not to dress, but throw their clothing into the fire. I would not let them eat, but made them sit while everything burned. Later, I made them walk to the river. They were still wearing some clothing, which I made them remove before I forced them to enter the water.

I pushed the canoe to the water's edge and got in. I made them swim near me as we went downstream. After a few hours, they asked if they could go ashore. I told them if they went to shore I would shoot them. I made them stay in the water even after nightfall. I kept them swimming all night. When we came to rapids, I made them go through them while I carried the canoe below them.

The next evening, I saw Leaf on the shore. I could see that there were two men standing beside her. When I pulled into shore and beached the canoe, she introduced them as members of her tribe. I asked her if the men in the water were the ones who had attacked her and she confirmed they were. They begged me to let them come ashore, but I refused, even though Leaf asked me on their behalf to do so. I told her they were lucky to be alive and I would not change my mind, nor would I kill them.

That night she told me she did not want me to be with her when she returned home. She said that she could not bear children and wanted me to be able to have them. I argued that it made no difference to me. It was then that she told me that she was inflicted with a disease that one could get only when they mated. She knew there was no cure for it and that it was just a matter of time before she would suffer the effects of this scourge.

I knew this disease could flare up, then disappear, only to reappear later, usually leaving one blind or deaf or with some other impairment. Needless to say, I was distressed with this news. She was adamant and refused to hear any argument from me. She and the two men from her tribe left me the next morning. I looked at my prisoners and wondered if they would get this disease, as they both had raped Leaf. But no matter, I would make them swim as long as I wanted them to or else.

I had a meal, but I refused to feed them, or let them out of the water. I got into the canoe and made them swim alongside again. Late that afternoon the older man, who was now a blue color, begged me to let him go ashore. I agreed, but left him sitting on the shore, while the other man and I continued on. The second man begged me to let him go ashore, but I refused. All that night he begged and cried.

The next morning we continued on. I paddled very little because the river current carried the canoe along. It was also easier for the remaining swimmer.

It was obvious that my prisoner's worst discomfort was the cold, and he had weakened considerably. Just before noon, I could hear a waterfall ahead of us. The current was getting stronger, so I allowed the man to go ashore. I, too, paddled to shore and, taking a big stone, smashed a hole in the front of the canoe and pushed it out into the current. It was soon swept over the falls. I left the man sitting where he was on shore, while I went below the falls. I could not see the canoe.

I continued on. Two days later, I came to the White Man's village. I detoured around it until I was once again in the Mohawk village. I was well received and enjoyed their company once more.

I was carefully questioned by an Elder, who advised me to continue on to other Mohawk villages to the south. There were different types of White men in that area who were not very friendly with the ones in this area. So after spending a few days in this village, I left. I headed south, crossing the big river.

Getting across the river to different islands was not difficult. There were many canoes going back and forth among them. The Mohawk village was on an island, and I soon found a canoe going that way. I followed the big river upstream until I came to a large river which flowed into it from the south. I knew by following this river upstream I would come to a large lake. This lake was known as Mohawk Lake.

When I reached the extreme southern end of this lake, I realized that I was not far from the village of my grandmother. I did not feel safe in going to her village, so instead went toward the salt lake which I knew was not far away. After several weeks I came to the salt water and went south along the coastline.

29. By the Salt Water Lake

Soon I came to a large village on an island where there lived a large colony of White people. These people wanted furs like the French, but gave more for them. I was given a job loading the furs onto a large canoe with big white sails and many guns along the outside. The work was hard, as the bundles of furs were very heavy. I had to walk up a small narrow plank to get on the boat and then go below to a large room where the bundles of furs were stacked to the roof.

We were given trade goods for our labour, which we in turn had to trade with other Indians for food and things we needed. It was beginning to turn cold, so I had to find suitable lodging before the snow fell. There came a slack period when the canoe that was expected to arrive did not, and so we had no work.

I decided to go further south because another Indian had come from there and said there was another race of White Man who were more generous than the ones I had seen so far. I had no desire to return to the village near the French which was the Mohawk village called Hochalaga.

I left before the snow came; although it was cold, I had sufficient clothing and food for a few weeks. There were many villages and many different tribes, all Iroquois: Seneca, Oneida, Cayuga, Onondaga, as well as Mohawk. They had no quarrel with me as long as I did not take furs. I went out of the territory of the Iroquois, south to the land of the Delaware. I was told they would not bother one lone Indian.

I traveled by the water's edge as much as possible, but soon had to go inland because of so many bays and inlets. There were also large swampy areas where one could not cross. I met many Iroquois tribes as I went south, but they did not bother me as long as I was not trapping for furs. Soon I came to the Delaware area. These people were related to the Iroquois so did not bother me, but I was not welcome to stay too long in each camp.

30. More White People

There were more White Man villages the further south I went. The first ones I encountered were Dutch people who spoke a very harsh tongue, but were friendly. I was told that if I had been with a large group of Indians they would not have been so friendly.

I now came to an area where the land was made up of rolling hills and valleys. One day I came to a lake that was so beautiful that I sat by the shore admiring it. I heard footsteps, and an older Indian came and sat by me. He said nothing for a few moments and then asked me where I was from. I told him where I had come from and he told me he was from a small tribe that lived by a river flowing into the lake about an hour's walk away.

He invited me to accompany him to his village and because he was so friendly I accepted his invitation. He said he was of the people called the Chickahominy and these were part of a larger group of tribes with various names. He told me later that I had passed many of these when I traveled south from the Delaware area. These were friendly people and I had no need to fear for my safety. The people south of his tribe called the Powassen could be troublesome.

We arrived at his village and I was surprised to see how orderly they had placed their lodges. The whole area was clean and the people were well-dressed. I was welcomed and given a place to rest. They were treating me a little too well and this made me suspicious, but I accepted their hospitality with caution. I was to learn that these people treated everyone in a friendly manner and were very open-hearted and generous.

That night we sat in a large lodge with a firepit in the centre. I think the whole tribe was there to see the stranger. They wanted to hear the stories I could tell about my travels and how other tribes were coping with the intrusion of the White people. I told them frankly that I had not come into contact with any tribes who had any problems with the White people, but they did show concern about the numbers of these people that were coming.

They told me that they and other people to the south were having great difficulty with these people, as they were just taking their land without consideration of the people already there. This land was usually the best land for gardens in the valleys. They cleared great areas of forest and built large villages for their people.

Many of the natives were killed and their women used by the White Man. As they spoke I could see their anger rising. We talked long into the night and by morning my head was spinning with their tales of bad treatment by the White men. I had heard such stories before, but had not seen these things happen. I told them about my own problem with the White man I had worked for and how it came about that I had killed him. I did not say that I had also raped his wife, if it could be called rape. To me it was just getting what he had taken from me.

They gave me sympathy for what I had been forced to do, because they realized that I was not a violent man. I didn't tell them that I had killed several men, although they were Indians and I had good reason to. But killing was not the Indian way; rather, negotiations and consultations were the norm to settle problems. These people had tried to talk with the White Man and when they had come to an agreement, the White people would promptly break it.

We spent several evenings by the firepit listening to each other's stories and I found it to be enjoyable. One morning a group of White people came into camp and I could see them talking with the chief and elders of the tribe. I was told by an elder that they had a child missing from their village not too far from the Indian village and were there seeking help to find the child.

The chief and elders lost no time in gathering as many men as were available within the village to help look for the child. I volunteered to help even though I was unfamiliar with the area. The leaders accepted my help and wisely put me with a young man of about twelve years old, who I was to learn knew the area very well.

When we arrived at the White Man's village we were given different areas to search. The young boy I was with decided to look in a specific area that he knew well. He had gathered berries there many times. We followed a well-traveled trail for most of that first day and made a camp by a small stream. The next morning we went on in a direction decided by my young companion.

We followed the stream until the boy stopped and listened but I could hear nothing except the birds singing. He turned away from the stream and went along a steep, heavily wooded ravine. I kept silent because he appeared to know exactly what he was doing. He suddenly stopped and pointed to a large overhanging outcrop above us.

Asking me to stay where I was, he put his excess gear on the ground and began to climb a steep incline. Soon I heard him talking to someone and an angry cry was his answer. He returned to where I was standing and told me the lost child was in the overhang above but would not come down.

He realized the child could not understand him as he could only speak the Indian language. He asked me to try to get the child.

I climbed the steep hillside; it was very difficult with loose gravel and no footholds. Finally I reached a ledge below the outcropping and I could see the White child cringing against the wall. I spoke to him in a soothing voice speaking what English I could. He had a wild-animal look in his eyes like a cornered deer with no way to escape. I decided it best not to force him out of his place as we could both fall and injure ourselves.

I climbed down to my companion and told him we should wait for a while. I then proceeded to make a meal for us. I lit a fire so as to create a smell of cooking food in the air so if the lost child was hungry he might come to us. The food we had was dried meat and berries but I threw some of the meat into the fire to make it look like it was being cooked.

My companion realized what I was doing, since he, as most Indians, had experience with lost people, especially children. People who are lost for a time sometimes go slightly mad and can injure themselves and the people who try to help them. In this case we were also Indians and he feared us more than if we were White men.

We ate our food and waited. Before long we both heard a slight sound from the brush nearby. We lay on the ground and acted as though we were about to sleep off our heavy meal. Soon the White child approached and, when close enough, seized the food left out for this purpose and began to wolf it down. I sat up and smiled at him and he ignored me while he ate.

Neither I nor the Indian boy said a word and when the child was done we offered him drink and he accepted. He then lay upon the ground and went to sleep. I raised him and placed a fur beneath him and one on top of him. He slept until it was dusk and then awoke with a start and was about to flee when I put my arm around him and held him close.

I could tell that this boy was no more than three or four years old. He began to struggle then thought better of it and relaxed, realizing we were there to help him. We prepared more food for us all and then we went to our furs to sleep. The White boy slept close to me for security.

The next morning I told the White child who we were and that many people were looking for him. I told him we were taking him home to his parents that very day. He seemed to understand what I was saying and did not object.

After a small meal we left in the direction of the village. That night we had to sleep again in the forest, but would make the village the next day.

As we approached the White Man's village I had the white child on my shoulders since, because of his size, he could not keep up to us. Many times I had to duck overhanging branches to avoid the child banging his head, but we made good time. Most of the village was out looking for the missing child so no one saw us until we were about halfway through the gate.

A woman gave a great shout and soon the whole village present were there around us. The boy's mother took him from my shoulder and they held each other closely, both crying. I and my companion were taken to one side by an older man and questioned about where we had found the child. We gave him all the details and he had some of the women prepare a meal for us.

Word went out that the child was found safe and returned to his mother. Soon the village filled with White people and Indians. The White people wanted to show their gratitude to me for saving the child but I would have none of it. I told them I was a stranger visiting the Indian tribe nearby and the young boy I had with me deserved their thanks, not I.

They gave the young man many gifts and tried to express their thanks in many ways. Many years later they also showed their thanks by taking most of the lands around the Indian village, leaving the Indians with little more than the village proper. But at this time their thanks were genuine.

We returned to the Indian village of my hosts and the rescue of the White child was talked about for many nights by the firepit. The gifts given to the young boy were looked over many times. They consisted of White Man's clothes that could fit the boy and some metal pots and containers that could be put to some use but unfamiliar to the Indian.

I stayed there for more than a week, mainly because they were so friendly and the village sat in such a beautiful place. But one fine summer morning I left. My new friends were sorry to see me leave and gave me directions to the next village. I went to the southwest for several days, following the stream that ran by their village, till I came to a trail that led me into the territory of the Monacan tribe.

31. Attacked by White Men

I followed this trail until one day I smelled wood smoke and knew someone was nearby. I came upon a thing I later learned was called a wagon. I had not seen anything like this before—it had a box with four round spoke things that I could see it rolled on. It was covered with a cloth on large hoops and was open at the back.

I was so busy looking at this strange object that I was taken by surprise when two White men seized me and threw me on the ground. They tied my hands behind my back and set me against a tree. Women and children came from the bushes and looked at me. One of the men asked me if I could understand him.

His language I knew to be English and I was familiar with it. With my arms bound I could not make gestures to show what I was saying. I indicated as best I could that I could understand somewhat. He then asked me what I was doing around their wagon. I tried to tell him that I had never seen one before and was just curious.

He slapped me hard across the face and told me not to lie to him as he knew I was going to steal something like all the other damn heathens. I tried to explain that this was not my intention, but it did no good. He hit me with his fist and the other man began to beat me also. I lost consciousness and when I came to I was still against the tree, but darkness had fallen.

One of the woman saw that I was conscious and told one of the men. He came over to me and said that I was just another goddamn Indian and he would take care of me in the morning. To say the least, I was more than surprised by what had happened. Never before had I been treated like this. What had I done to receive such treatment? They left me there in confusion. It turned cold and I was in some pain from the beating I had received.

I thought and thought and could not explain my predicament. Soon one man came over and checked my bonds and was satisfied I could not escape. They kept the fire by their wagon going all night. One man guarded the camp and kept the fire stoked. Toward early morning I heard a very slight sound behind me and a soft whisper nearby telling me to stay still. I could feel a sharp knife cutting the bonds behind my back and I pretended to be asleep. Looking over to the man on guard, I could see that he was dozing, so I slipped behind the tree and melted into the darkness.

I had not gone far when a voice told me to follow him. When we were far enough from the camp we were joined by a large group of Indians, who began asking me questions and why I had been beaten and tied by the White people. I told them my story and that I was at a loss to explain why they had taken me. They left me with two other men and the main party left in the darkness.

Around midday a man returned and told us to follow him. I did with difficulty, but managed. We came to the camp where I had been held and to my surprise the two White men were now bound to the same tree I had been hours before. The women and children were huddled together in fear, and some were crying.

The leader of the Indians asked me if they were the two men who had beaten me and I said they were. He then asked the White men why they had done this to me and they said it was because I was a thief prowling around their wagon. They asked why they thought this was so. One man said that all Indians were thieves. This made the leader so angry he struck the White man across the face.

"You who have come to our country and stolen our land and women and you call us thieves!" the leader exclaimed. "You have taken one of our people and beaten him for no reason. For this you shall pay."

Turning to the other of his people, he ordered the two White men to be punished by our methods. One man was untied and the leader told him to pick an opponent from among us. He was confused by what the leader meant him to do and the leader explained he was to get the same treatment he had given me. But as we were civilized people he could pick the man to give him his punishment and could defend himself.

The man carefully selected one who he thought he would have no trouble with. But to his and even my amazement the man he picked was a very good fighter and beat the White man until the leader told him not to kill him. The White man was in terrible shape but he would live.

The other man then had his turn. He chose another man but the same thing happened. Both had been beaten carefully, not hit enough to put them unconscious, but enough to do considerable damage to their features. They were a bloody mess with many broken bones.

The women and children had watched what was happening to the men and cried out when they saw what the results were. They feared that terrible things lay in store for them. The women expected they would be raped and tortured and the children stolen or killed.

The leader said to the women, "We do not fight women, nor do we rape White women as the White men do to ours. Take your men and dress their wounds and remember this day." He then ordered his men to destroy everything the White people had with them. They set fire to the wagon and everything else, except the clothes the people were wearing. They took nothing for themselves.

We stood and watched as the women helped their men to the stream. After the fire had burned itself out, we left them. We went to the north again and by nightfall had covered a good distance. Afterwards the firepit was lit, some food was prepared, and we ate. Soon after, an older man came and dressed my wounds. Luckily no bones were broken, but my face was badly swollen.

They gave me a fur and left a place by the firepit for me to sleep. I did sleep like I had not slept since before coming to the White man's camp. There was a sense of security with these people who had befriended me, so I knew I was safe and I could sleep soundly.

I awoke in the morning and helped as best I could to make a meal. When we had finished eating, the leader began to question me. I told him my story from the time I left the Delaware territory. They listened carefully to what I said and then the leader told me they were from the west and were Shawnee people.

I had heard of the Shawnee, but thought they lived too far away for me ever to meet them. They seemed like good people, but I had heard they were very unpredictable in their behavior. I had no choice but to keep a friendly smile on my face and I did appreciate what they had done for me. They told me in no uncertain words that I should avoid their territory and then they quickly broke camp, leaving me alone by the firepit.

I had to make up my mind which way I wanted to travel and soon decided that I was better off to go northwest to the Susquehanna area and avoid the White people here. I left following old trails and keeping to the low country as much as possible.

After about four days of walking, I met some Indian people who turned out to be the Susquehanna and they were friendly to me. I had met them before when I was going the other way. They told me the White people were numerous along the edge of the salt lake, which they called the ocean, and I would be well advised to go further north.

A few days later I came to a small village of Indians by the Susquehanna River who were in an uproar. I was told that a small village of about two hundred White people near them had taken one of their men prisoner. They had accused him of killing a White man and were putting him on trial in the White Man's court. I decided I was going to leave this place as soon as I could.

I had no interest in becoming involved in this matter. But things did not work out that way. I was asked if I could speak the English language and before thinking the question over I answered that I could. The Chief then asked me to act as his interpreter at the trial of the Indian involved. I could not refuse or I would have been in very deep trouble.

The Indians did not dispute the fact that their tribal member had killed the White man but they thought he was justified in what he did. His accusers said that he just killed the White man for no reason. The Indians claimed that the White man had raped and killed the accused Indian's wife.

The Indian story was that the accused, named Lone Wolf, had just gone through the ceremony of making him and the killed woman man and wife. They had made a temporary lean-to by the fork of a nearby stream and he had gone to fish. When he returned he caught the White man strangling his woman and had killed him with his battle axe. He had gone to the White Man's village to explain what he had done and had been arrested.

The White Man said that there was no evidence that this is what happened. They said the Indian had buried his woman and burned the lean-to and this contradicted what the Indian had claimed.

The trial was to begin the next day and we arrived at the White Man's village early. We were shown to a building where the trial was to take place. It was a large room with a table at one end and a chair placed at each side. There were benches for spectators in front of the table.

It was fortunate that we had arrived early. There were about fifty of us Indians and this took most of the benches available. There were some chairs to each side of the table in the front where the accused was to be held, for soldiers who were the police in the town. The man sitting as judge was a sargeant of the army, dressed in his dress uniform with its red jacket and gold braid.

There were about twenty-five British soldiers billeted in the village and they had the task of keeping law and order in the area. This was their law, not the Indian's.

The Chief sat in the front center and I was at his right side. When the trial began the judge asked that the charge be read. He then asked who was defending the accused. The Chief stood up and said, through me, that he was.

The judge said he was not recognized in the White Man's court and he gave him ten minutes to find proper representation. The Chief was plainly bewildered, but I was not, and asked the other Indians if they knew any of the White people.

Looking around, they saw one person who had been to their village and had shown an interest in Indian culture and ways. It turned out this man was the teacher of the only school in the area. He told me that he had no experience with this sort of thing and I told him we Indians were lacking experience also. He laughed and agreed to try to do his best. The Chief agreed with my choice and we were ready.

The judge again asked who represented the accused and the teacher said he did. The judge now asked that the Indians clear the courtroom before the trial was to start. I explained this to the Chief and he stood up and spoke to the judge. Actually he told me and I translated what he wanted said to the court.

"You have accused one of my people of a crime and now you will not let us be present while you judge him. This we will not accept. This I say to you, there are many of my people who live in this area and they are angry. Around your village are more than fifteen hundred warriors waiting for me to leave your village. If I do not by a certain time they will attack. If I consider your law is not fair they will attack and not one of your people will survive."

I was surprised because I had not seen one warrior, but I said nothing. The judge had plenty to say.

"How dare you come into our court and threaten us. Do you think you can scare us this way? My soldiers are ready to defend this village and are on guard at this very instant."

The school teacher stood and asked that the threats stop and the trial begin.

A soldier reported that he had attended to the scene of the crime and could see no evidence of a murder victim, only the dead White man who was brought back to the village.

The teacher asked the Chief about this matter and had the Chief sworn as a witness. On the stand the Chief said, "We too went to the area where you claim there is no evidence. Our trackers found where your soldiers had buried the girl and we removed her. We found bite marks on her neck, chest and breasts, and these had been bleeding which meant they had been inflicted before death. She had also been raped and strangled. All this we can prove. It was your soldiers who had destroyed the true evidence."

The judge was now a purple color. Raising his voice in anger, he told the Chief to leave the room. As the Chief returned to his chair the judge said, "This proves nothing, as it is well known that Indian women are not very moral; consequently the girl deserved what she got."

The Chief went to the place where he had stood before as a witness and said, "What a mockery of English justice this is. You, the judge, have been known to the Indians for a long time because you attacked a small village of Indians two years ago and killed all the women and children there.

"You have been a marked man for some time and revenge will be ours some day. There will be no rest as long as you are in our area. I and my people will leave here now, but if we do not have the prisoner released to us by sundown this village will perish. What you have said about our women deserves no answer."

With that said we left the village but remained in the clearing where the villagers could see us waiting. About an hour later five soldiers on horses came out of the village but were turned back by some warriors who threatened them with rifles.

I had time to look around and as far as I could see there were no fifteen hundred warriors about. This was a very serious bluff by the Chief and could end up being a bad thing for me. After all, this was not my problem; but of course I was wrong—this was the problem for all Indians in these times.

Tension seemed to mount as the time was running out but thankfully just before dark the village gate opened and the prisoner walked out. He was greeted with much joy by everyone. The Chief cautioned everyone to stay on guard and do no celebrating until we saw what the White Man intended to do.

In the days that followed, the White Man's village was strangely quiet. The neighboring Indian tribes began to assemble and made a show of strength to the White Man. One day a troop of about fifty soldiers arrived, causing us a lot of concern.

Then one morning the school teacher and an officer of the British army appeared at the village. He asked to see the Chief and the Elders. He informed them that their tribesman was cleared of all wrongdoing and that the army was moving the twenty-five soldiers who had been present to another territory much further to the west. This was good news to the tribe and that night there were many celebrations.

I made haste the very next morning to get out of this territory as fast as I could. Some of the White people were still angry and would seek revenge, I was sure. I headed to the land of the Erie. These people were related to the Delaware and were known to be friendly to the Iroquois. I must mention that in my travels I passed many abandoned Indian villages that had suffered great losses to disease. This was evident by the large number of burials. I came across many camps in the back forests where all the people had died and I had to bury many of the those poor people. It is impossible to describe the effect on the Indian of the terrible diseases the White people spread among us.

The weather was now very cold and snow was falling as I walked through the forests. I kept to the well-used paths and met many Natives but no White people, other than traders, whom I avoided.

After six weeks, I came to the land of the Erie. I was made welcome to stay in one of their villages. Each day when it was possible, I went out to hunt and fish for food. I wanted to support myself and have plenty to give to my hosts for the warm lodging they provided. Most of our spare time was spent talking around the firepit about the White Man and how they were affecting our lifestyles.

When spring finally arrived, I was anxious to be on my way again. I was sick of longhouse living, with the smells and fleas. Leaving my new friends, I went east toward the Wenro area. I now planned to go to the Mohawk country to live out my life there. I had no reason to expect that these people would not accept me. If there were any of my grandmother's people left, I hoped that they would welcome me.

32. Again I Work for a White Man

My first encounter with the Wenro was with a group which was led by a White man. This man had a very friendly face and the bluest eyes I had ever seen. I learned that he was Dutch. He made me welcome when he was told I was a Mohawk. He plied me with questions about my trade experiences with the French and English traders. He told me he was going to open a trading post near the Seneca nation and asked if I would accompany him.

I agreed, and the next morning we left, going to the north. The Indians with him had been friendly toward me and left to return to their own village. I went to a Seneca village and managed to get enough help to carry the many boxes the Dutch trader had. We went to a village on a small lake to the north. I was told this lake had a wide and high waterfall where the water fell down to the next lake.

The Iroquois League below the great lakes was made up of five different tribes, as I have mentioned. Since the Mohawk were on the northern end and the Seneca on the southern end, they had become better warriors, not because they desired this, but because they were the first ones the enemy would make an attack on.

The Seneca were suspicious of the White man I was with and watched him very closely. But because of his friendly appearance and actions, he slowly became accepted and his trading post thrived. He was much more generous than the other White people were. One thing was that he had no Black Robes with him to try to make us believe in another God before we could trade.

I worked hard for the trader, and he gave me many trade goods and treated me with respect. Soon I was helping him to bargain with the other Indians and was sent into the country around us to get the Indians to come to our post.

Although I was accepted as a Mohawk, this was not Mohawk territory. This area was held by another tribe of the same nation as the Mohawk—in other words, they were also Iroquois. Not being of this tribe, I was still able to come and go, as long as I did not hunt for furs to trade with the White Man.

Even if I had not been Iroquois, I would still have been able to move about freely. It must be understood that most tribes were happy to see people from other nations. They brought with them news and stories to be told around the firepit at night. Even people from tribes who were known enemies were made welcome, if they showed themselves to be friendly.

It is wrong to think that all the Indians did was fight one another. This is far from the truth, as before the White Man came most disputes were settled by negotiations by the Elders to everyone's satisfaction. People who left the village during the summer months were glad to see other people. They had no other way to gather news. We at the trading post had no trouble getting the latest news, for this was a place where people gathered.

This was, in effect, why the White Man was allowed to travel where he wanted. The Indian could see benefit in allowing him to do so. Too late, they realized the Whites were not just visitors, but were becoming permanent residents. Even then, they did not object, because they felt obliged to share as they had always done among themselves. They felt there was enough space for all.

One evening when I was with a small group of people near the great falls in the river, a member of another group came and told us his tribe had been attacked by French traders by the lake below the falls not far from where we were.

A group of men was soon formed to go and help these people. We went inland for awhile then turned toward the lake, keeping where we could hear the sound coming from the falls to our left. We did not arrive at the camp until noon the next day and it was a terrible sight.

The lean-tos had been burned and most of the people were dead. An old woman, still alive though dying, managed to tell us that the attackers had come in three large canoes with a few Indians from a distant tribe. They had been welcomed because her people thought they had come to trade, but the White men had instead attacked the unprepared Indians.

The people had no chance to defend themselves. After killing the men, the White people seized the youngest girls and raped them repeatedly. In fact, they had taken some of the girls with them when they fled. We did what we could for the old woman but it was useless. We buried the bodies of the people and, leaving some older men to clean up and do the proper ceremonies, the rest of us took off after the Frenchmen.

We knew that their canoes would be heavily loaded and they could not make much speed. We also knew they would camp on the shore of the lake on our side, because the lake could be treacherous with heavily loaded canoes. We went along the shore and soon came to where they had camped.

We knew these were the people we were seeking, because of the footprints of White Man's boots and the marks on the shoreline where they had pulled up the heavy canoes. The firepit was cold, so we knew they had gone on and were at least two days ahead of us. We continued on until after dark and made no fire that night, because it could be seen from far away.

The next day before daylight we were on our way again. This was new territory for me, so I just followed the others. They left the lakeside and went a few miles inland which I could not understand, until one of them told me the lake shore curved inland a few miles ahead and we were taking a shortcut.

Just before nightfall I smelled wood burning and realized it must be from the Frenchmen's fire. We could hear the lake and see the glow in the sky from their firepit. It was decided that two men would get as close as possible and keep watch on them and the rest of us would sleep. We would attack them before they moved about in the morning.

Before daylight we heard the two men returning and they took us quietly to the White Man's camp. They were just beginning to move. We attacked quickly and quietly and they did not know what had hit them. It was over very soon. The three White men as well as their Indian guides lay dead.

We searched for the girls we knew they had taken and found them by some shrubs, bound together. We cut them loose and assured them they had nothing to fear. Some of the girls knew the men with us. One girl suddenly sprang up and ran into the forest. I ran after her and caught her before she went too far. I grabbed and held her and I could feel her panic. I realized she was only about thirteen years old.

I carried her, struggling, back to camp and the others laughed when they saw us. They could not understand her panic until they realized that this girl was not one of theirs. The other girls managed to quiet her down and she told them she was from the Onondaga tribe which was near the Cayugas. The placement of the Iroquois tribes were the Seneca, the Cayuga, the Onondaga, and then the Oneida, and finally the Mohawk.

She had been taken by the Frenchmen from a camp after her family had traded with them. She had been getting water from the lake when the French left and one had grabbed her and forced her to go with them. She told the other girls she had been raped repeatedly by the one young Frenchman we had killed.

We left the dead people where they lay and some of our people took the canoes back to their own camp, while the rest of us, along with the girls, retraced our steps to the camp. It took us three days to reach the camp where the men lived.

The people were glad to see us since they had been informed what had happened and they were concerned for the safety of their menfolks. They knew the French had guns that could kill from a distance. They quickly took charge of the girls and made them welcome. For the next few days they held ceremonies for the girls' relatives who had been killed.

They made arrangements to return the girls to their own tribes and this made the girls happy. But the girl from the Onondagas did not want this. She did not want to return to her own people, as she was shamed. Her people were very moral and as far as they were concerned they would consider her to be spoiled goods and no man would take her for his woman. She felt her life was ruined, even though it was no fault of her own.

The people I was with were Cayugas and they did not want the responsibility of the girl and asked me to take her to the Seneca area where the trading post was located. I was hesitant to do this, but since we needed the good will of these people I agreed.

I made plans and left in two days' time. The girl had become very pleasant and now appeared grateful that she had been rescued. She had been given clothes and shoes to wear. She said nothing for the first while on the trail, but paid attention to what I said. I was now in my middle thirties and getting on in years, so I took my time getting to the trading post.

33. I Get to Know Yellow Flower

The girl told me her name was Yellow Flower and was so named because when she was a baby she was a yellow colour and the medicine man had worked hard to change it. For some reason this condition happened to many of this tribe. Her parents lived in an area that had many hills and valleys and she told me it was a very nice place to live.

I could tell that the girl was really homesick and felt sorry for her. I tried to reassure her that all would be well for her, but I wasn't too sure myself. The girls in our tribe, as with hers, matured very young. Many girls and boys were made man and woman or man and wife by the time they were fourteen and some earlier.

In Yellow Flower's tribe the girls were encouraged to marry as soon as they entered puberty in order to discourage them from experimenting sexually with boys. Usually the marriage was arranged long before the girl grew up. If the girl was unfortunate enough to experience what had happened to Yellow Flower, the boy was no longer committed to marry her and this brought great shame on her family.

This seemed to me to be a very restrictive group and I told the girl that this was not the way in my tribe.

I told her we were free to select our own mates and that we were sexually active as soon as we were ready, as nature dictated. She thought this was a terrible custom and said she could never live under those conditions.

When we arrived at the trading post the White man was glad to see me and welcomed the girl, after I explained what had happened to her. He was very kind to her and gave her a place to live in the post near me. He made it plain that I was to look out for her and make sure she was safe. I must say that I expected him to take advantage of her as other White men did with Indian girls, but to his credit he never did. He was more like a father to her and showed her much affection but never made a sexual advance.

I spent many hours with Yellow Flower, and she proved to be intelligent and very independent. Her family had been hardworking and close. Her mother had a sense of humour that kept the family laughing about the simplest things. Being named Yellow Flower was a case in point. They were very moral people and kept the tribe's ceremonies without question.

The Onondaga occupied the land in the centre of the Iroquois Nation, and it was here that they had the Sacred Firepit and The Sacred Tree of Life, where all Iroquois were expected to attend ceremonies sometime in their lives. Here also was the central council of the Iroquois Nation, which ran the affairs of the whole people.

Over time I told Yellow Flower the story of my life and she found it interesting. She questioned me about everything and I realized she was a very naive person seeking answers because she had lived a sheltered life. I respected her and did not bother her in any way, which was unusual for me.

It was not long before she found herself to be pregnant. She went into a state of depression because she realized that the White man who had raped her was the father. Both the Dutchman and I tried to console her, but to no avail. I thought she was going to do away with herself and kept a close eye on her.

She perceived this and asked me why I bothered with her as she was a shamed woman among our people. I told her it was not her fault she was in the condition she was in and told her it made no difference to the people of most tribes. I knew in truth that most Indian men shunned a woman who had a half-breed child but did not tell her this.

In the meantime, the trading post prospered and the White man was very pleased. It must be noted that all trade was not made in furs, though it was the biggest part. The women of the tribes traded other things for goods. These were moccasins, plain and beaded, doeskin jackets, which were in great demand, high leather moccasins for winter use, leather leggings, and even gloves, fur hats, and tools.

The White man hired other Indians to carry the goods to the salt water post in large packs to be put on the great ships. He usually accompanied these trips and left me in charge of the post because he had come to trust me not only as an employee but as a friend. I returned that friendship with honesty.

It was during one of his trips away that Yellow Flower gave birth to a boy. He was healthy with a pale colour, so it was easy to see that he had White blood in him. His mother accepted him, but reluctantly at first. In time she realized it was not the child's fault and gave him the love a mother should.

34. We Become Family

When the child was about a year old, Yellow Flower and I became man and woman. I always felt that she accepted me because I accepted her and she had nowhere else to turn. I was considerably older than she was, but it seemed to make no difference to her. I was a good provider and I loved her son and took him as my own. He was a fine healthy boy that any father would be proud of.

We had problems mating at first because she would freeze up and cry when I went near her, but over time and with love and patience she came around and we had a good relationship. It was soon after this that she became with child again. As this was the first child I had fathered that I was sure of, it made me very happy.

Things had changed drastically for the Indian in the past few years. There were more White people than ever. Some White women had joined their menfolk. The hunters had to go further afield to get furs. The animals could not keep up with the White Man's demand for their pelts. Many Indians were giving their furs away for alcohol and becoming addicted to it.

About this time it became apparent that the English were replacing the Dutch and, as it came about, our trading post was taken over by the English. They were a little easier to negotiate with and luckily our trader was a very good man. He had a woman with him and a young son.

He asked me to stay with him with my family and I agreed. I had built a substantial lodge near the post by the forest so it was convenient for me to stay. I did no hunting except for meat for our table and to trade for other food. I was paid fairly well and managed to trade what I earned for other things we needed.

Yellow Flower gave birth to another boy and he was as healthy as his older brother. It was obvious to see he was a full-blooded Indian, not like his brother. Yellow flower never had any more children but I considered myself lucky to have such fine sons.

The boys grew quickly and were a great joy to us both. They worshipped their mother and she them. The years had gone by so fast that I never realized that I was now an old man of forty-two years or thereabouts. I knew I was giving the boys more chores to do because I didn't have the stamina to do them.

The older boy was broad in the shoulders and thin at the waist. He was very strong and handsome. His younger brother was built the same, but did not have his good looks. They never went through any ceremonies such as those for becoming a man, because the older brother, being a half-breed, was not acceptable to the tribes that lived around us. So the younger brother refused to have them.

We had named the older boy Cold Eyes because that is exactly how he appeared. His eyes were cold and calculating. The younger boy was named Slow Bear which was an apt name as he was slow and methodical. These two made a good pair.

There was an older Indian who hung around the trading post and was given odd jobs about the place. He was an intelligent man and I gave him the task of teaching the boys Indian ways. He taught them well and soon they supplied the post with all the meat we could eat. The old Indian was called Leather Skin because he had such a tough hide. He was a Delaware Indian, whose homeland was to our south, but for some reason that he never explained, he preferred to live among the Seneca. They accepted him as he was.

The two boys, seeing so many canoes, decided to try to build one. They asked Leather Skin to help, which he agreed to do. They went to work gathering willow branches the length and thickness Leather Skin told them he wanted. He took the boys out to the woods where they gathered the bark to cover the canoe. It was to be a long, hard project.

He then instructed them to cut the willow into the size of slats that he required. He then had them find a sapling to make the keel for the canoe. They found one the shape and size he wanted. They had to make tools of a certain type to cut the wood properly. The trader supplied them with small and large axes and various size knifes which were very sharp. He also gave them a proper stone to keep the tools sharp.

It took a considerable time to lay the keel properly and this tried the patience of the boys, but Leather Skin was in no hurry, wanting everything done right the first time. While they laid the keel they had a large container of water boiling madly over a fire. Into this they placed the willow ribs so they could be bent without breaking. In the meantime, Leather skin was busy showing them how to make the gunnels and the keel stays. They soaked leather thongs in water so they stretched when they tied the wood parts together. The leather when drying made the knots so tight they could not be undone. Leather Skin had previously damaged the bark on the pine trees and the sap formed on these cuts. This sap was collected and used as a glue. It hardened into a resin-like material.

Leather Skin had placed two spreaders in the centre of the canoe about three feet apart between the gunnels. Later these were to be used to help carry the canoe by tying the paddles to them and when the canoe was upside down on the man's shoulders the paddles rested there with his head in between.

They had notched the keel where the ribs were to be placed. They had a double gunnel each side and the ribs went between these. When they were ready, they took the willow ribs from the hot water and bent them to the shape required and placed them about two inches apart.

This part of the job took them a full month to do. When they were finished and it had dried to the shape desired, they started to place the bark covering on the ribs. This took them more than two months to complete because they had to gather more bark. Yellow Flower and two other women helped with the bark covering, sewing the pieces together with leather thongs and gut from the deer. They gathered the sap from the spruce trees. The spruce trees had little bubbles of sap on their trunk and it was an easy matter to puncture this bubble and catch the sap in a bottle. The bottle had to be as airtight as possible because the sap would evaporate and become hard.

When the sap was too hard to spread they mixed some of the White Man's liquor with it to make it more fluid. They poured the sap onto the bark covering and with their hands spread it evenly over the surface. They did this until a hard shell covered the ribs. It took over three months to finish the canoe and they then had to make paddles.

Leather Skin took the boys to the forest again to find the proper cedar tree to make the paddles. He finally selected one and after they cut it down, he had the boys cut a knot-free section the length of the paddles they wanted. After this he had them split into two pieces the portion that was cut off. He made each boy carry one piece back to the camp.

He set about carving these into paddles, with the boys helping when they could. He made the blade first and then the handle. When he was finished, they had two paddles exactly the same size and shape. They were light and strong. He made the boys rub bear grease into them until they shone.

Yellow Flower decorated the canoe with paints made from certain plants and had the paddles done in the same way. Now came the time to see if the canoe would float and carry two people.

The boys carried it between them to the small lake nearby. With Leather Skin standing in the water to steady the canoe and give final instructions, they got in. The boys knelt in the canoe as instructed, and Leather Skin pushed them on their way. There was much wobbling for awhile, but they soon found how to balance themselves properly. Leather Skin was proud of their work.

During the next few weeks the boys almost lived in the canoe. Cold Eyes finally returned to his chores while Slow Bear stayed in the canoe every day. Even he finally had enough and from then on the canoe was used only when required.

As the boys grew older, I noticed a difference in them and Yellow Flower also brought it to my attention. Cold Eyes had begun to take on more of the White Man's ways, while Slow Bear became more in the Indian way. Not that there were any conflicts between them, because they loved each other very much. Cold Eyes wanted to become educated so he could read and write and speak good English. Yellow Flower insisted that when we were together we were all to speak our native language. Cold Eyes did not object to this as he wanted to retain his Indian language also. But in and around the trading post he spoke only English, though with an accent. He would in later life lose this accent.

Leather Skin lived nearby, but we had never really looked to see where. One morning the boys told me they were going to build him a new lodge. I wondered about this and went to see where Leather Skin lived. I was suprised to find him living in a rough lean-to against a granite outcrop. It had seen better days and was badly constructed to begin with. I wondered why a man who could build such a fine canoe had a problem building a suitable lodge.

I went with the boys and together we spent the next few days building a more suitable lodge for Leather Skin. We built it closer to the trading post. He lived here for the next three years and then, as suddenly as he had appeared, he disappeared. We missed him and felt badly that we had not found out more about him.

As the boys grew stronger and bigger, I realized I was becoming weaker. I had developed a cough that persisted, regardless of the medicine I was given. I had fits of coughing that left me weak and drained. It became apparent that I had the lung disease brought to our land by the White people. Some people managed to get well from it, but most died. All you could do was rest and eat well and let the disease take its course.

During the next few months I did some work, but I had to rest often. When I had a fit of coughing, I brought up blood, a sign that I had not long to live.

Yellow Flower kept me away from people as much as possible. I would sit in the sunlight for hours, which seemed to make me feel better. Yellow Flower and the boys knew that my life was ebbing away and, with the trader, they made plans for the future. The trader would continue to support them if the two boys would help at the post and supply them with fresh meat. This arrangement took a great weight from my shoulders as I wondered how they would survive without me.

It came about that the older boy Cold Eyes worked more in the post, while the younger boy Slow Bear did the hunting. Both boys seemed pleased with this arrangement, as it was what they wanted to do. The trader and his wife began calling Cold Eyes an English name, James, which seemed to please him.

Soon I was too weak to even leave my furs and I lay there waiting for the end. It went on for months like this. Then one spring morning Yellow Flower tried to move me into the sunshine and I started to cough.

I coughed until I went unconscious. I must have lain there like this for some time. I was aware of people around me at times. Then one evening I went into a deep sleep and was thankful, for I was at last away from the constant need to clear my lungs, and I slept peacefully, away from the cares of this life.

The End

About the Author

George McMullen was born in Woodbridge, Ontario, on January 14, 1920. Seeking to avoid ridicule, he kept his psychic gifts secret from the public until he was in his forties.

In 1969 he began working with J. Norman Emerson, Ph.D., an anthropologist/archaeologist at the University of Toronto. Until Dr. Emerson's death in 1978, the two men did research at various Indian sites in southern Ontario, Ohio, and New York state. Dr. Emerson described McMullen's work in numerous papers delivered to professional groups. Many of these papers, along with commentary and personal insights, are compiled in McMullen's second book, *One White Crow*.

McMullen has traveled internationally extensively, working with research groups including the Edgar Cayce Foundation and the Mobius Group. His work is prominently featured in explorer/author Stephan Schwartz's two books *The Secret Vaults of Time* and *The Alexandria Project*. He continues to work with archaeologists, criminologists, and psychic explorers. He and his wife Charlotte live in British Columbia.

McMullen's unique first-person saga of life as a Huron began in his first book, *Red Snake*. *Running Bear* continues the story, told by Red Snake's grandson.

Hampton Roads Publishing Company
concentrates on three related areas of interest:
Metaphysical
Alternative medicine
Visionary fiction.
For a copy of our latest catalog, call toll-free,
(800) 766-8009, or send your name and address to:

Hampton Roads Publishing Company, Inc.
134 Burgess Lane
Charlottesville, VA 22902